A GHOST
IN THE WINDOW

OTHER BOOKS BY BETTY REN WRIGHT

The Summer of Mrs. MacGregor
Christina's Ghost
Ghosts Beneath Our Feet
The Dollhouse Murders
The Secret Window
Getting Rid of Marjorie

A GHOST
IN THE WINDOW

Betty Ren Wright

HOLIDAY HOUSE / NEW YORK

Library of Congress Cataloging-in-Publication Data

Wright, Betty Ren.
A Ghost in the window.

Summary: A man who died in a car crash after
allegedly stealing $50,000 from a bank, tries to
communicate with his family through Meg's dreams.
Sequel to "A Secret Window."
[1. Dreams—fiction. 2. Extrasensory perception—
Fiction] I. Title.
PZ7.W933Gf 1987   [Fic]   87-45331
ISBN 0-8234-0661-X

For Delores Draper *and*
for Ethel Mae Greene

A GHOST
IN THE WINDOW

1

"So what did you think I was going to try out for, the beautiful Native American princess?" Rhoda Deel leaned back and peered out from under her visored cap. "You'll get that part, Meg, want to bet? You looked fantastic up there on the stage. And you did the lines fairly well, too," she teased. "Maybe a little quivery, but . . ." She tipped her hat back with an index finger. "I guess *I* didn't quiver, did I?"

"You sounded like somebody's horrible little brother just begging for trouble." Meg's eyes were on the sunlit theater-on-wheels, where tryouts for this summer's play continued. She couldn't imagine wanting to play a mischievous ten-year-old when there was a beautiful princess in the cast of characters. But then, Rhoda seldom did the expected. That was one reason it was such fun having her for a friend.

"You like to make people laugh, and I'd rather give them goose bumps because I'm so brave," Meg murmured. "How'd we get to be friends?"

Rhoda grinned. "The world needs us both. Actually, it's not that I *want* to make them laugh. But since I look like a boy, sort of, I might as well make the most of it. Four feet ten, skinny, short red hair and freckles. Does that sound like your typical Native American princess?"

Meg touched the long black braid that she thought of as her trademark. "Just because I have dark hair, that doesn't mean I look like Princess Running Deer," she said. "But I want that part, Rho! I really do!"

She could picture herself slipping into the pioneer settlement to warn her white friends of the brutal attack that was coming. And in the second act there was that wonderful, heartbreaking speech in which the princess said goodbye to the settlers before returning to her own people and certain death. If Meg's voice quavered when she read the lines, it was because the fate of the princess had moved her. To do the right thing and then be punished for it was dreadful.

A slim blond girl moved to the center of the stage and began reading the princess's farewell speech.

"Yellow-hair no good for princess," Rhoda muttered. "Why waste time?"

Meg bit her lip. "But she *is* good, Rho," she whispered. "Oh, darn, listen to her—she's the best yet. You can tell she's acted before. And they won't care about her hair—she can wear a wig, you know. Mr. Cody said we should let the costume and makeup people worry about how we looked."

They were silent for a couple of minutes while the girl finished the farewell speech and then, at Mr. Cody's suggestion, turned to an earlier scene and read some more. Finally Rhoda cleared her throat. "Meg Korshak did it better," she intoned, under her breath. "Big Chief Deel—Big Deel, that is—has spoken."

Meg tried to smile. She hoped Rhoda was right, but her confidence was slipping away. And she wanted to be in this play more than anything she could think of. If Rhoda got the little boy's part, they would have a marvelous summer, going to rehearsals together, traveling to playgrounds and parks all over Milwaukee to perform, sharing the excitement of being in a real play. "I suppose I could work on costumes or sets or something," she said slowly. "If you get a part and I don't, I mean."

The blond girl finished reading and returned the script to the director. Meg narrowed her eyes against the sun, trying to read his lips.

"I think he told her she was terrific, Rhoda. Maybe he even told her she had the part."

Rhoda stood up and stretched. "He told her she'd find out who gets what as soon as the tryouts are over. Same as he told you and me. It could take hours. Come on, Meggie, let's get an ice-cream cone at Darys' and go home. I think I'm about to have sunstroke."

Meg followed her friend across the small park to the bus stop. Rhoda was right. Mr. Cody had their addresses and telephone numbers. There was no reason to sit around and brood about how good everyone else was.

Later, walking down Brookfield Avenue and licking her double-dip chocolate-chip-and-mocha cone, Meg began to feel a little better. It was going to be a good summer, whatever happened, mostly because she and Rhoda would be together. Trying out for the theater-on-wheels production had been Rhoda's idea. If they didn't get parts in the play, they were going to check with the museum and the art center to see what kind of summer activities were scheduled. Rhoda had even suggested a way they could earn some money. They would ask their apartment superintendent if they could wash cars in the underground parking garage. It would be fun working together, and Meg's mother and Rhoda's father would have to approve of a job that kept them in spending money and could be performed without leaving the building.

At the thought of her mother, Meg's lips tightened. Lately, she and her mother didn't agree on anything. *No, not just lately,* she amended. It had been that way ever since her parents' divorce became final a year ago. During the months before that, with her father up in northern Michigan, living in Uncle Henry's cottage and working on his stories and articles, Meg had kept insisting that someday he would come back to them. Someday soon! When he didn't, her mother seemed to look around for someone to blame. That was when the problems began. Hardly a day went by now without a sharp disagreement between mother and daughter.

"Maybe you remind your mom of your dad," Rhoda had said one night, after Meg had poured out her hurt feelings. "You're sort of—sort of different—like he is. And maybe you look a lot like him. Do you?"

Meg sniffed. "So what if I do? That isn't my fault. Besides, I'm glad if I look like him. I love him! He's still my father, and he writes to me often and . . ."

She'd subsided into grumpy silence. Her brother, Bill, had said much the same thing as Rhoda when she'd complained to him about the way her mother treated her. "I don't think Ma's over the divorce, Meggie," he'd said. "What I mean is, she doesn't want to be married to Dad anymore, and yet she can't forgive him for going away. When she looks at you, I guess she sees him."

"Then maybe she doesn't want me in the family anymore either," Meg muttered.

Bill turned suddenly unsympathetic. "Now, that's just dumb," he snapped. "Ma loves you, kiddo. She'd feel rotten if she heard you say that."

"But she loves you more," Meg insisted. "She practically never gets mad at you."

"I try not to say things that'll upset her," Bill had retorted. "Unlike some people I could name."

Remembering that conversation, Meg promised herself she would do nothing to spoil this summer. She would be tactful. She wouldn't argue. She would be an even-tempered, dependable, feminine version of Bill.

At least, she'd try.

Rhoda swallowed the last of her cone and grabbed Meg's elbow. "Hey, we're home," she said. "You look as if your head is a million miles away."

"I was thinking about my mother," Meg said. "If we do get parts in the play, she'll probably say it's silly or a waste of time."

Rhoda sighed, wiped sticky fingers on her jeans, and pulled open the big glass door that led into the apartment foyer. "Think happy," she advised, swinging the door wide and bowing. "After you, Princess Running Deer."

Someone was humming. Meg stopped, startled, just inside her apartment, before she remembered that this was Wednesday, her mother's afternoon off.

"Is that you, Mama?"

The humming stopped. "I'm in here." The voice was her mother's, but it had an unfamiliar lilt. Meg hurried down the hall.

The usually neat master bedroom looked as if a gust of wind had blown everything out of the closet and onto the bed. Dresses, jackets, skirts, blouses, the old blue bathrobe—all were scattered over Grandma Korshak's flower-garden quilt. Her mother stood in front of the mirror, examining herself critically.

"What's happened?" Meg demanded, suddenly uneasy. "What are you doing?"

Mrs. Korshak smiled into the glass. "Taking inventory," she said with something very like a giggle. "Trying to decide what's needed."

"Needed for what?"

"I had a telephone call this morning. An incredible one!" Her mother turned away from the mirror and snatched a blouse from the bed. "It started me thinking—I haven't bought any clothes since—for ages. And my hair is a mess. . . ."

Meg scowled. A telephone call? What was this about, anyway? Her mother was acting like—like a *girl*. She was like a girl getting ready for a date!

An alarm sounded in Meg's head, warning her not to act as outraged as she felt.

"Who called?" she asked, trying to make the question casual. It was probably one of the salesmen at the real estate office where her mother worked. Meg hated him, whoever he was.

"I'll tell you about it when Bill gets home," Mrs. Korshak said. "No use going through the whole thing twice."

The whole thing! Meg retreated to her own bedroom, her stomach churning. Had her mother been seeing someone for a long time without telling them? If so, why was she ready to admit it now? Suddenly, anything seemed possible.

For the next half hour Meg lay curled up on her bed, trying to think about the play, about Princess Running Deer, about the car-washing job—trying to ignore the humming that had begun again in the front bedroom. When the apartment door finally opened, she was on her feet in one bound and racing down the hall.

"Where've you been?" she scolded her brother. "I thought you'd *never* get here!"

Bill looked surprised. "Hey, I'm home early," he said mildly. "What's your problem?" His eyes were intent behind his glasses. "Did you get the part you wanted in the play?"

"Don't know yet."

That was Bill. With all he had to think about—his pre-med studies at the university, his summer internship with the pharmaceutical laboratory—he didn't forget what was important to her. He really cared. For the thousandth time, at least, Meg thought about how lucky she was to have him. With Bill for a brother, her family could never fly apart completely.

Could it?

"Mama has something to tell us," Meg whispered. "She wanted to wait until you got home." When Bill didn't say anything, she rushed on. "I think maybe she's going to get married."

Bill dropped his lunch box on the hall table. "Married! Ma? You're crazy."

"No, I'm not. She's in her room looking over all her clothes and smiling at herself in the mirror and talking about taking an inventory. . . ."

Bill brushed past Meg and strode down the hall. He stopped in the bedroom doorway and looked at the jumble of clothes on the bed. Meg peeked nervously over his shoulder.

"Hey, what's going on?" He grinned at their mother, but Meg heard the tightness in his voice. "You cleaning out your closet?"

Mrs. Korshak folded a skirt over the back of a chair. "Not cleaning, just sorting. I think it's time I bought some new things."

"Any special reason?" The tightness was more pronounced. Meg clenched her fists so hard that the nails bit into her palms.

"As a matter of fact, yes!" Their mother's face glowed with pleasure. "I'm going on a trip."

"A honeymoon!" Meg gasped. She knew Bill heard, because she felt him stiffen.

"Would you believe," Mrs. Korshak went on, "your uncle Bill—he's the one you're named for—called me at work this morning! He's coming home on leave from his bank job in Rome, and he wants me to meet him in New York for a reunion. All expenses paid! Everything!" She slumped into a chair, as if the excitement were more than she could stand. "We'll spend ten days sightseeing in Manhattan—he has a little bit of business to attend to there—and then we'll fly to Pittsburgh for ten more days, to visit the rest of the family. Isn't that marvelous?"

"Marvelous," Bill agreed, smiling at Meg. "When are you leaving, Ma?"

"Bill will get to New York this Sunday, and he wants me to fly in Monday evening. I have to talk to my boss, but I have the time coming, and we're not very busy, so . . . what's the matter with you, Meg? You look as if you've been let out of jail or something. Are you *that* glad your mother's going away?"

"Yes—I mean, no—I mean—" Meg rolled her eyes. "I'm happy you're going to have a vacation, that's all. I mean, I'm happy that it's just Uncle Bill—"

Her brother's elbow caught her squarely in the ribs. "We're both happy for you, Ma. You deserve a change."

The telephone rang, saving Meg from having to explain any further. She raced to answer, hoping it was Rhoda calling. Rhoda's parents were divorced, too, so she would understand exactly how Meg had felt when she thought her mother might be getting married again.

But it was a man's voice that answered Meg's breathless hello. For a moment, she didn't recognize the smooth baritone.

"Meg Korshak? This is Jim Cody from theater-on-wheels."

Meg froze. "Yes," she said. The word was a squeak.

"I wanted to tell you that you have the part of Princess Running Deer, if you want it. Your reading this afternoon was exceptionally good."

"Oh." Meg's cheeks burned. "Oh, thank you! That's — that's terrific!"

"We're going to start rehearsals next Wednesday at Humboldt Park. You'll get your copy of the script then." He hesitated. "You still there?"

"Yes, yes, I am. I'm just so glad —"

Mr. Cody chuckled. "That's all set, then. I'll see you Wednesday at the Humboldt Park lodge. And remember, we start promptly at ten."

Meg cleared her throat. "Did Rhoda — could you tell me if Rhoda Deel got a part, too?"

There was a shuffling of papers at the other end of the line. "Short redheaded kid? Yes, she did. She's going to be Joey Martin. She made a better little boy than any of the boys who tried out. I'll call her next, if she's a friend of yours."

They said goodbye, and Meg stood very still, holding the telephone and listening to the murmur of voices from her mother's bedroom. Everything was all right — oh, much, much better than all right. Everything was perfect! She was going to be Princess Running Deer and Rhoda was going to be the mischievous little boy. And she didn't even have to wonder whether her mother would consider the play a waste of time, because her mother would be away for three weeks, enjoying a much-needed vacation. By the time she returned, the play would be in full swing, and it would be too late to criticize or complain.

Meg floated back down the hall, trying to decide how to tell her own big news. *Guess what, Mama and Bill, I'm going to be—*

She stopped at the doorway. Something had changed. Bill looked worried, and her mother's familiar frown was back.

"Good news?" Bill asked quietly. When Meg nodded, he reached out and tugged her braid. "You got the part you wanted. Congratulations, kiddo." But he didn't smile.

Mrs. Korshak didn't seem to hear. "I was just telling Bill how we'll arrange things while I'm gone," she said. "You realize you can't stay here alone for three weeks, Meg."

Meg stared. "I won't be alone. Bill will be here."

"He'll be at work all day. It won't do at all."

"But where will I go? What are you talking about?" Meg could feel Bill's eyes on her, willing her to stay calm, but she couldn't help herself. "Grandma Korshak can come here and stay—she'd be glad to."

"Grandma Korshak hasn't been feeling well for weeks," her mother said flatly. "We're not going to ask her to pick up and move into town. Not when you have a father who's perfectly able to take a little responsibility for his own daughter."

So that was it. Meg turned her back on Bill. "I *can't* go away," she wailed. "I can't! I have the lead part in the theater-on-wheels. We start rehearsing next week."

Her mother scooped up an armful of clothes and

moved to the closet. "Well, I'm sorry," she said. "It's too bad you have to miss some fun, but it can't be helped. Your uncle Bill is coming home to this country for the first time in years, and I want to see him. There'll be other plays."

Meg felt as if she were going to explode. "I won't go!" she roared.

Her mother whirled, her face pink with anger. "Oh, yes, you will, my girl," she snapped. "You're going to stay with your father, and that's all there is to it. We'll call him tonight and tell him you're coming!"

2

*It is like no place Meg has been in before. The entrance is
narrow but widens quickly. Along the sides are gleaming
white stakes, their sharpened points reaching toward her. She
is filled with horror as she realizes the stakes are giant teeth.
When she looks upward, she discovers more teeth threatening
her from overhead. She is walking into a huge mouth!*

*Ahead, light slants through long slits in the walls. Gills,
she thinks. I'm inside a fish, like Jonah in the Bible.*

*The thought of the old Bible story calms her for a moment.
Jonah didn't die in the whale. But as she moves into the dim
cavern of the fish's mouth, she becomes increasingly fearful.
She won't die in the fish, but something bad will happen
there. Something bad . . .*

"Meg, wake up. Rhoda's on the phone." Mrs. Korshak's voice cut through the dream and brought Meg
upright in bed. She was in her own room, with sun
pouring through the window. A garbage truck
clanked and grumbled in the street below. The giant

fish was gone. *But it was one of the real dreams,* Meg thought, and she shivered in spite of the mid-June sun. Grandma Korshak called the real dreams a secret window into the future. Grandma had them, too, and she considered the window a special gift. But she didn't dream about a monstrous fish with a gaping, hungry mouth. . . .

Meg jumped out of bed, eager to put time and space between herself and the dream. She would tell Rhoda about it, she decided. Maybe Rhoda could think of an explanation for a fish big enough to swallow a person.

Her hand was on the hall telephone before she remembered she had much more than the dream to tell Rhoda about. Memories of the furious scene in her mother's bedroom the day before came flooding back. It had ended with Meg rushing into her own room and slamming the door behind her. She'd stayed there all evening, had even refused the Korshak King Kong Klub sandwich (bologna, Cheddar cheese, tomato, pickles, and mustard on rye bread) that Bill brought to her door at about nine. The summer was ruined, absolutely destroyed by some dumb old uncle whom nobody had seen or heard from for years. And by Meg's mother, of course.

"Hi, Rho." Outrage made her voice tremble, and Rhoda noticed at once.

"What's the matter with you? I thought you'd be up at dawn doing Indian love calls out your bedroom window. Mr. Cody told me you're Princess Running

Deer. Congratulations! I wanted to call you last night, but my dad came home early and we went out to shop and have hamburgers."

"Congratulations to you, too."

There was a pause. "Something's wrong, right?" Rhoda said slowly. "How about meeting me on the steps?"

"Something's wrong. Right." Meg sighed. "I'll see you there as soon as I get dressed. And have breakfast," she added, suddenly aware that she hadn't had anything to eat since the ice-cream cone on the way home from the tryouts. What a long time ago that seemed! Before she thought her mother might be getting married again. Before Mr. Cody's telephone call. Before the announcement that Meg was to be shipped off to stay with her father, whether she wanted to go or not.

In the bathroom she splashed cold water on her face and stared into the mirror. Maybe, she thought, her father wouldn't want her. Maybe he just wouldn't have time for a visitor this summer. He might flatly refuse to let Meg come, and she would be able to stay home and be Princess Running Deer, no matter what her mother wanted. How would she feel, though, if her father said she couldn't come? She snatched a towel and buried her face in its soft folds.

The smell of warm chocolate filled the kitchen when Meg was ready for breakfast. Her mother was making brownies, one of Meg's favorite foods.

"Feeling better this morning?" Mrs. Korshak asked brightly, as if nothing were wrong. "Did you sleep all right?"

"I had a bad dream." Meg sat down at the table and filled her bowl with cereal. "Is Bill up?"

"Up and on his way," her mother replied. "That boy has more ambition than any three kids I've ever met. He said to tell you he'd be home from work fairly early, in case you wanted to—to talk." Mrs. Korshak sounded uncomfortable, as if she were wondering why Meg would want to confide in Bill rather than in her mother. *The reason is,* Meg answered the unasked question, *that what we usually talk about is you. And sometimes,* she added, *my dreams.*

Bill and Rhoda were the only people besides Grandma Korshak who knew that Meg's dreams often came true. She'd tried to tell her father about the real dreams once, long ago, but he'd changed the subject, after warning her never to talk about such things to her mother. Mrs. Korshak didn't believe in what she couldn't explain, Meg knew that, and she knew her father didn't like problems. He wouldn't say so, but he'd rather people kept their worries to themselves.

There was silence in the kitchen while Meg ate her cereal and her mother lifted the brownie pan from the oven and set it on the edge of the sink to cool. "I want you to know I'm sorry you're going to miss that play,"

Mrs. Korshak said. "Bill tells me it's something you really want to do."

Bill tells me. Meg scowled. *I told you myself, but you don't listen to what I say.* "I have the lead part," she muttered. "I'll never get a chance like this again."

"Never is a long time." Mrs. Korshak began cutting the brownies into squares.

"I can stay with Rhoda," Meg rushed on desperately. "She wouldn't mind."

Mrs. Korshak shook her head. "Certainly not. Rhoda's father has all he can do raising a daughter by himself. He works long hours, and I'm sure it worries him to leave Rhoda by herself so much. I'd never ask him to be responsible for you, too." She paused. "I said I was sorry. There's just nothing I can do about it."

Except let me stay home where I belong. Aloud Meg said, "Maybe Dad won't want me to come right now."

"I talked to him last night," Mrs. Korshak said, without turning around. "He'll meet you at the bus station in Trevor Monday afternoon."

Meg pushed her cereal bowl away. That was it, then. She was going. In spite of her resentment, she felt a thrill of relief that her father had been willing for her to come. She wondered if there had been a big argument before he'd said yes.

"You'll have a good time," Mrs. Korshak said. "Maybe you'll make nice new friends."

Meg didn't bother to answer.

"Do you want a brownie? They're still warm, but—"

"No, thanks." Meg stood up and carried her dishes to the sink. "Rhoda's waiting for me downstairs."

"Maybe she'd like a brownie."

Meg paused at the door. "I don't think so," she said. "She has a good part in the play—a little boy—and she won't want to put on any weight."

It was a ridiculous thing to say; Rhoda never put on weight. She could probably eat fourteen banana splits in a row without gaining a pound. But Meg wanted her mother to know that baking brownies didn't make up for spoiling a summer. Two people's summers— Rhoda was going to be terribly disappointed, too.

Feeling only a little guilty, Meg hurried from the apartment.

"It's no use making a big fuss, Meggie," Rhoda said. "Believe me, it never works."

Her first response to the news had been to lean back on the apartment steps and pull her visored cap down over her face. Meg waited, thinking how different this morning might have been. *We'd be doing something to celebrate. A bike ride, maybe. Or a picnic. Something neat.*

After a minute or two, Rhoda sat up and pushed the cap to the back of her head. "It never works," she repeated.

"I'm just so mad," Meg groaned. "It was going to be a perfect summer."

"Well, being in the play won't be much fun without you," Rhoda said thoughtfully. "Maybe I'll pull out, too." She twisted a red curl, weighing arguments for and against quitting. "No, I might as well stay in," she said finally. "I don't have anything else to do. But it won't be the same. I'm really sorry you have to go away."

It was like Rhoda to take bad news calmly, consider all sides of a question, and end up worrying about someone else's disappointment as much as her own. "They decide what you're going to do," she said now, without explaining who *they* were, "and you might as well go along with it."

"I know."

"Of course," Rhoda went on, "that isn't always bad. My dad decided we were going to move to Milwaukee. I hated to leave New York, but if we hadn't moved, I never would have met you." She grinned. "You'll only be gone about three weeks, right? There'll be a lot of good stuff we can do when you get back."

Meg nodded.

"And you'll get to see your dad again," she continued. "That'll be nice. He's living in a cottage on Lake Superior, isn't he? You can work on your tan."

"It's my great-uncle's cottage. He's letting my dad stay there and look after it." In spite of herself, Meg's spirits began to rise. Then she remembered the other thing she must talk to Rhoda about, and she shivered.

"I had one of the real dreams last night," she said. She described the dream—walking inside the giant fish, the feeling of dread—and Rhoda listened intently.

"Who wouldn't be scared?" she said when Meg had finished. "Inside a fish, for heaven's sake!"

Meg shook her head. "That's the strange part, Rho. It wasn't only the fish I was afraid of. I mean, I knew something else—something scary—was going to happen if I kept on walking."

"The monster fish swallowed a monster octopus just before it swallowed you," Rhoda suggested. "Right around the corner eight long arms were waiting to—"

"It's not funny, Rhoda," Meg said. "Not if it's going to come true."

"You're sure it was that kind of dream?"

Meg nodded. "It was very bright, the way the real dreams always are," she said. "I can't exactly describe the difference, but I always know which ones are going to come true. I wrote this one in my dream book before I came down here."

Rhoda sat up straight. "Okay. But there has to be an explanation. I mean, maybe the fish represents something else. Something you're worried about."

"Maybe." Meg stood up. Rhoda had made her feel better about going away but she wasn't going to be of much help in explaining the dream. There was no use talking about it. Meg would just have to wait to see what happened. After all, she was going to be staying with her father on the shore of the biggest lake in the country. . . .

"Fish don't come *that* big in Lake Superior," Rhoda said slyly. "Don't worry about it when you go swimming with your dad."

Meg snorted. "Are you a mind reader or something?"

"Don't have to be," Rhoda said cheerfully. "I know you pretty well."

That was the truth, and it was another reason why Meg didn't want to go away from home, even for a short time. She liked being with people who understood her—Rhoda and Bill—people who could guess what she was thinking and feeling before she told them. Her father wasn't like that; he had been away for so long that she felt as if she hardly knew him. His letters asked lots of questions but didn't tell much, and his occasional visits, while the divorce was being settled, had been hurried ones.

A disturbing thought struck her. What if she didn't recognize her father in the Trevor bus station? It was a scary idea—worse even than the thought of meeting a giant octopus inside the stomach of a monster fish.

3

Meg leaned back and tried to Think Cool. The air conditioning had broken down just after the bus left Green Bay, and the temperature had been mounting ever since. She thought of double-dip ice-cream cones (with Rhoda, who was getting farther away every second). Swimming in Lake Superior (icy-cold all year round, according to her father). A glass of soda (last night, in the kitchen with Bill. He'd pretended to be envious because Meg was going to spend three weeks lying on a beach, soaking up sunshine while he slaved in a laboratory.)

Think Cool. An ice pack (her mother, nursing a headache on the living-room sofa this morning, while Meg finished packing her suitcase).

Meg shifted on the hot vinyl seat, remembering how Bill had stalked into her bedroom after breakfast and closed the door behind him. "Look," he'd said, "Ma's out there making herself sick because she feels guilty about sending you to stay with Dad. Tell her it's okay."

Meg rolled her red bathing suit into a ball and dropped it into the suitcase. "It's not okay," she snapped. "Why should I pretend it is?"

"Because this'll be the first vacation Ma's had in years, and you don't want to spoil it for her."

Meg glared at him. "What about *my* vacation? Why do I have to make everybody else feel good?"

Bill gave the long black braid a tug. "Because you're basically a not-bad kid," he'd replied and left her fuming.

Eventually, she'd gone to the living room, as he'd known she would, and said she hoped the next three weeks would be a fun time for both of them. Her heart wasn't in it, but a few minutes later she'd heard her mother go to the kitchen and empty the ice pack into the sink.

A fun time, she thought. *Like now, for instance, riding in an overheated oven, with nothing to look at but endless miles of trees.* Occasionally the bus caught up to a car pulling a trailer or a boat, its back seat loaded with suitcases and children and sometimes a dog. Meg looked down at them wistfully. Once in a while the children would wave, and she waved back. She wondered if they knew how lucky they were, going on a vacation trip with both their parents, and nothing to think about except having a good time.

The old lady in the aisle seat sat up suddenly and

looked at her watch. "Twenty minutes to Trevor," she announced, as if that were the best news in the world. "I can hardly wait! I feel as if I've been away a year instead of just ten days."

Meg forced a smile. "My dad says it's a nice town."

"Oh, it is!" Her companion tucked wisps of hair under a net that was studded with tiny beads. "Of course, in summer it's very crowded—don't say I didn't warn you about that. My boy Junior has a sporting-goods store—makes a ton of money, I can tell you. The tourists come from miles around to buy their camping and fishing supplies and get souvenirs and all. Sometimes you can hardly walk down Lakeview—that's our main street."

"I won't be staying in town," Meg said. "My dad and I will be at a cottage on Lake Superior."

The old lady twisted to look toward the back of the bus. "Is your father sitting back there somewhere?" she asked. "Why didn't you say so? We could have exchanged seats. I don't care where I sit, just so I get home."

Meg looked down at her folded hands. "I'm meeting my father in Trevor."

"Oh?" The old lady sounded curious, but Meg didn't explain. She hated telling people that her parents were divorced. Risking rudeness, she leaned back and closed her eyes, pretending a sleepiness she didn't feel.

She must have dozed off, because suddenly the bus

was slowing and the old lady was gathering her belongings into her lap. "This is it," she said proudly, when Meg opened her eyes. "My Trevor! Don't say I didn't tell you it would be crowded. Just look at that, will you!"

The bus wheezed and groaned around a corner and threaded its way between cars parked on either side of the narrow main street. Meg stared in astonishment at the throngs of people on the sidewalks. "It's like— like a carnival," she murmured.

The old lady frowned. "If you mean everybody's having a good time, that's true," she said primly. "But when the tourists go home at the end of the summer, Trevor is a very quiet town. I like it both ways."

Meg nodded, wondering if she'd said something wrong. She concentrated on the signs over the shops —THE SQUIRREL'S NEST and THE WISE OLD OWL. The biggest store had long metal tubs lined up in front of its windows.

"That's my Junior's place," the old lady announced. "Those things out front are freezers for fish, in case you're wondering. Tourists bring their best catch in and leave it there for people to admire. Then they pick 'em up on the way home. You wouldn't believe the size of some of those fish."

Meg shivered. The fish in her dream would have been as long as that whole store. Longer! She thrust the thought away.

"There's the bus station, right on the corner," the

old lady continued. "It's the storefront with the crowd on the sidewalk. Folks here to meet friends, I suppose." She leaned across Meg and waved vigorously at a huge man wearing a visored cap with TREVOR lettered on it. "That's my Junior, come to meet his mother. Which one is your father, dear?"

Meg discovered that she couldn't breathe. There was no one in the crowd who looked familiar—no tall, thin man with a dark beard and glasses. What if he was standing right there—maybe with his beard shaved off—and she didn't recognize him? Or what if he hadn't bothered to come to meet her?

She slid down in the seat and tried to look unconcerned. "He might—he might not be here," she stammered. "He might have an appointment or—"

The door of the bus station opened, and a tall, bearded man stepped out, squinting into the sun.

"There he is!" Meg shot up. "He just came outside."

"Well, that's fine." The old lady struggled to her feet. "You two have a good time, now." She bustled down the aisle, leaving Meg to stare through the tinted glass at her father.

Of course she'd recognized him. How could she have worried about that? But she felt shy, as if he were a stranger. After all, this was the first time since he'd left home that she would be alone with him. On his visits to Milwaukee, he'd taken Bill and her out to dinner, and Bill had done most of the talking. College courses, new friends, part-time jobs—he always had plenty to talk about. Meg had sat quietly, pretending to herself that nothing had changed, pretending that her mother just happened to be working late, and soon Meg and Bill and their father would go home and they'd all be together again.

"Everybody out, young lady. This is as far north as you're gonna get." The bus driver sounded impatient, but his face was kind. Meg hitched her shoulder bag into place and hurried toward the door.

"Somebody meeting you?" the driver asked.

"Yes!" Meg stumbled on the top step and hurtled out of the bus, right into her father's arms. They hugged without speaking, and Meg pressed her cheek against his chest.

"I'll get your things," Mr. Korshak said after a moment. He edged his way to the side of the bus, where the driver had opened the luggage compartment. "How many cases?"

"One." Meg smiled at him, comforted by the discovery that she wasn't the only person who felt shy in this situation. Her father's arms had been strong and loving, but his heart had been beating very fast. Now he busied himself looking at luggage tags without waiting for her to point out which suitcase was hers.

When he rejoined her at the edge of the crowd, his face was red. "Car's up the block a way," he muttered. "Couldn't get any closer. Tourists are cluttering up the street." He began walking with long strides, and Meg scampered after him.

"The place goes crazy this time of year," he said, and he didn't sound as pleased as the old lady who had shared Meg's seat. "You should see it in midwinter, though. Like a ghost town most of the time. Nice."

Meg sidestepped to miss a collision with a fat man in shorts and a bright orange T-shirt. "Well, I guess it doesn't make much difference to you," she said. "The crowds, I mean. Uncle Henry's cottage is a long way from town, isn't it?"

Her father looked down at her and then away, as if the comment had startled him. "The car's right there," he muttered. "The blue sedan near the corner."

Meg was surprised. "I thought you used Uncle Henry's old truck."

"Had to get something of my own. I thought I told you when I wrote."

Meg recalled her father's last letter. *How are you doing in school? How's Rhoda? I hope you're helping your mother a lot. . . . I keep busy with my writing, and that's the way I want it. No big sales so far, but some interesting prospects. . . .* She'd kept every letter he sent her, but they had told very little about life in the north woods. Certainly he hadn't mentioned buying a car.

Mr. Korshak dropped the suitcase in the back seat of the sedan and waited for Meg to fasten her seatbelt before he pulled out into traffic. "We'll be turning off the main street just a block or so ahead," he said. "Then you'll see how the town looks the rest of the year. All the action's here on Lakeview."

"Do you have to get groceries before we go out to the lake?" One of the things Meg had wondered about during the long bus ride was whether her father would remember to stock up on important things like peanut butter and pizza and ice cream. She could imagine him thinking so much about his work that he forgot about eating. She didn't want to be without her favorite foods for three whole weeks if she could help it.

"No problem." They turned off Lakeview Avenue, and, as he'd predicted, the scene changed. Big old wooden houses and smaller shingled ones lined the street. The lawns were dotted with toys, and children rode their tricycles down the bumpy sidewalks.

Mr. Korshak swung the car over to the curb and parked in the shade of an oak. "This is more like it," he said. "This is why I like living in Trevor."

Meg looked around her. Was she supposed to admire this perfectly ordinary street? "But you *don't* live here," she said after a puzzled moment. "I mean, you just come into town to shop, right?"

Silence. Her father turned and looked right at her for the first time. "I'm awfully glad you're here, Meggie," he said. "It means a lot to me that you wanted to come."

Now it was Meg's turn to look away.

"But I'm afraid you're going to be disappointed," he hurried on. "I just hope—well, things aren't the way you think. There's more I didn't get around to mentioning in my letters—besides the car."

"What do you mean?" His nervousness was beginning to scare her.

"I don't live in Uncle Henry's cottage anymore. If you were looking forward to lying on the beach and hiking in the woods—well, I'm sorry."

Meg forgot her shyness. "What do you mean? Where do you live, then? Do you have a house?" She looked around again. "Is it one of these houses? Is that why we stopped here?"

"No, no, I just wanted to talk to you," Mr. Korshak said. "I moved into town about six weeks ago. To a house on Emerson Avenue, just a few blocks from here. And no, I didn't buy it. I don't have money to buy a house. It's a kind of a—a boarding house."

"A boarding house?" Meg couldn't believe she'd heard right. "You mean you live in a crummy old tenement with a bunch of strangers?"

Her father laughed weakly. "It isn't a crummy old tenement, babe, and they aren't really strangers. The house belongs to a very nice woman I've known ever since I moved up here. She's a nurse at the hospital, and she makes a little extra money renting out some rooms."

"But—"

Mr. Korshak sighed. "You *are* disappointed, aren't you? You wanted to stay at the cottage, and I don't blame you. It's beautiful out there. I guess I should have told your mother the whole story when I sent her my phone number, but I didn't think she'd be interested. Still, it's probably a good thing I didn't. She might not have let you come if she'd known."

Fat chance, Meg thought.

"Actually, I didn't have any choice about moving," her father went on. "Uncle Henry had a chance to rent the place for six months, and he didn't want to pass it up. I wasn't paying anything to stay there, you know —just looking after the place for him. . . . I'm sorry, Meggie."

Meg didn't know what to say. It wasn't just the loss of the cottage that disturbed her. She didn't want to live in one room in someone else's house, be part of someone else's family, for three whole weeks. Looking out the car window at the houses that lined the street, she envied the people who lived in them. They were home. That was where she longed to be, now more than ever.

"The Larsens—that's the name of the people I live with—are great," Mr. Korshak said coaxingly. "There's a boy sixteen or seventeen and a cute little girl. You'll have fun with them."

Meg hardly heard him. Where would she sleep in this boarding house? Would she have to share a bathroom with a houseful of strangers?

What if there were bedbugs?

Rhoda's voice sounded dryly in her ear, trying for a joke. *In case of bedbugs, sleep in a chair.*

But a boarding house! It was probably a dingy, dark place full of lonely people, like her dad, who had no place else to go. His expression, as he waited for her to say something, was that of a small boy who expected to be scolded.

Come on, Meggie. Don't be a drag. Now it was Bill's voice, pushing her to be nicer than she was.

Oh, well. She reached out and squeezed her father's hand. "Don't worry, Dad. We'll have fun. I'm really glad to see you."

The last part, at least, was true.

4

The house was big and old, but it was definitely *not* the crumbling wreck Meg had expected. White paint gleamed in the afternoon sun, and a rambling porch across the front and partway around one side offered inviting shade. Two little girls, one with straight yellow-white hair and the other with a cap of brown ringlets, played on the steps.

Mr. Korshak carried Meg's suitcase up the walk. "Hi, Steffi," he greeted the blond child. "This is *my* little girl, Meg. Meg, this is Steffi Larsen. And her friend Astrid."

Steffi hugged her knees. "She's not a *very* little girl," she observed with some disappointment.

Meg smiled at her. "I'm fourteen. How old are you?"

"Five." Steffi pointed at her companion. "Astrid's only four. We're playing out here because Mama's mad and Caleb's catching it."

Meg glanced quickly at her father, who had stopped at the foot of the porch steps. A woman's voice cut through the sunny stillness.

"—quit moping about something you can't change, for heaven's sake! You act as if—" The voice faded. Then the screen door flew open, and a long-legged blond boy burst out onto the porch. When he saw the Korshaks, he took a step backward, his face set in lines of anger and frustration.

Meg's father put out a hand as if to keep him from running away. "Caleb, this is my daughter, Meg. Meg, meet Caleb Larsen."

"Hi." They eyed each other somberly.

"I have to get going," Caleb muttered. "Stuff to do."

"Maybe you can show Meg around Trevor," Mr. Korshak suggested. "Not right now, but sometime. You'd like that, wouldn't you, Meggie?"

Meg felt herself blushing. Her father sounded as if he were talking to babies. And he was actually asking a boy to pay some attention to her—a boy who obviously wished he were a hundred miles away from this spot.

"Well, I'm pretty busy," Caleb said, not looking at either of them. "You know, I've got the delivery job, and there's a lot of chores to do around here."

Meg glared at him and then at her father. "I won't have any trouble finding my way around this little town," she said coolly. "If I want to, that is."

Footsteps sounded inside the house, and Caleb sprang into motion. He clattered down the steps, leaping over three dolls and a teddy bear to make his escape.

"I'm going to tell Mama," Steffi shouted after him as he catapulted onto a bicycle and skimmed away. "You nearly kicked Teddy. You could have *killed* him!"

The front door opened, and a plump woman in a crackling-white uniform came outside. Her skin glowed with good health, and her expression was pleasant but serious. When she saw the Korshaks she looked dismayed for a moment. Then she laughed.

"Meg, it's good to see you," she said, holding out a hand. "You've already met the rest of the family, I guess, though not at their best, I'm sure. I hope Caleb was civil. There's nothing like arriving in the midst of a family discussion to make you feel at home, right?"

"It wasn't a family discussion," Steffi protested. "Caleb was catching it."

Mrs. Larsen patted the smooth blond head. "Well, if he was, you don't have to enjoy it so much, miss," she said. "Come inside, Meg. You must be hot and tired after your long bus ride. We don't have very fancy accommodations for you, but I think you'll be comfortable. We're just very glad to have you here with us."

Something inside Meg, some tightly wound coil of shyness and resentment, began to relax. She followed Mrs. Larsen into the house, across a sunny entrance

hall and up uncarpeted stairs. Her father trudged behind them, carrying the suitcase and puffing a little.

"This is a nice house," she said as Mrs. Larsen led
the way down the upstairs hall. "I like it."

"I like it, too," Mrs. Larsen said. "And that's a good
thing, because I'll probably never be able to afford to
fix it up any better than it is right now. This is your
room." She turned in at the last doorway on the left,
then stood aside so Meg could enter. "It's the smallest
room in the house, but still . . . It used to be my husband's study, and after he died it became my sewing
room. I hope you won't mind the sewing machine over
there and the box of materials stored in the corner. The
daybed is comfortable, and I've emptied the two top
drawers of the bureau so you'll have plenty of room for
your things."

The smallest room in the Larsen house was bigger
than Meg's bedroom at home. The daybed was covered
with bright chintz, and sheer white curtains moved in
the breeze. The wallpaper was pale yellow, so faded
that the pattern had almost disappeared. In front of
one window a rocking chair held a battered stuffed
dog.

"The dog is Steffi's contribution to your well-
being," Mrs. Larsen explained. "Your father talked
about his little girl coming for a visit, and Steffi
wanted to make sure you had something to cuddle in
case you forgot to bring your teddy bear." She and
Meg's father exchanged smiles.

"The bathroom's right across the hall," Mrs. Larsen went on. "We only have the one up here, but there's a shower in the basement. There are just two other boarders besides your dad. Mrs. Tate has the room next to this one—she baby-sits for Steffi while I'm at work. And there's Jeff Townsend, but he's only here on weekends and often not then. He rents a room as a home base, but most of the time he's out on the road selling."

Meg's father dropped the suitcase next to the daybed. "I was hoping Caleb could give Meg a tour of the town," he said, "but he was busy. Maybe you and I can take a little ride before I leave for work, Meg. I'm on from four to eight, so we haven't much time, but I can give you a quick look."

Meg wondered how many more surprises he had in store for her. "Work!" she repeated. "Don't you do your writing here?"

"I'm not talking about writing. I mean the job at the newspaper—typing, billing, that kind of thing." He sounded a little impatient. "I'm sure I told you about *that*. Four hours a day, sometimes less, five days a week. It pays the rent and leaves plenty of time for writing the rest of the day." He hesitated. "I did tell you. You just forgot."

"You did *not* tell me." Meg was suddenly close to tears. "I'll never even see you."

"Of course you'll see me. What are you talking about?"

"I thought we would sit on the beach and talk. I thought we'd go for boat rides and swim and hike in the woods and——" She broke off, aware that Mrs. Larsen was looking from her to her father with an anxious expression.

"I've already said I was sorry I didn't tell you about moving out of the cottage," Mr. Korshak said, sounding annoyed. "But we'll spend just as much time together here as we would out at the lake, Meg. Wherever I am, I spend most of the day writing. You know the writing has to come first."

"You don't even care that I'm here!" Meg exclaimed. "If you really cared, you'd take time off so we could do things together."

"If I took time off, I couldn't send your mother money every month. I couldn't afford to live here. . . ."

They stared at each other. Remembered words filled the sewing room—words Meg had never wanted to hear again. *Writing is the most important thing in my life.* That was what her father had told them two years ago. Bill insisted it didn't mean he'd stopped caring about them, but Meg wasn't so sure. He had left, after all. He had just walked out with little but his typewriter and his ambition to be a successful writer. He'd left early one morning, without even saying goodbye.

Now he was practically saying those terrible words again. *You know the writing has to come first. . . .*

"I have to be on my way to work," Mrs. Larsen spoke softly, apologetically. "I don't always work second shift, but we have a flu epidemic among the staff, and I have to fill in where I'm needed."

"You owe Kathy an apology, Meg," Mr. Korshak said. "She's gone out of her way to make you feel welcome, and all you can talk about is Uncle Henry's cottage."

Mrs. Larsen brushed the words away. "She doesn't owe me a thing, Jim. I understand how she feels, and I'm sure you'll find ways to be together while she's in Trevor. I'm sorry I won't be home for dinner on your first night with us, Meg."

Kathy and Jim. Meg picked up the stuffed dog from the rocking chair and went to the window, willing them both to leave her alone. "I'll unpack now," she said. "Thank you for showing me around, Mrs. Larsen."

"You're very welcome, dear." No-nonsense heels clipped down the hall and descended the stairs. Meg knew her father was still there, waiting for her to say something, but she stayed at the window. She didn't want to talk to him. Why should she?

The silence stretched out unbearably. "Meg, I meant it when I said I was glad you're here," he said. "It's important to me. I want you to have a good time."

"I'll be okay." She sounded sulky, self-pitying, even to herself. Bill would be disgusted if he could hear her, and so, probably, would Rhoda.

"I'll be home by eight-fifteen," her father promised.

"That's one good thing about a small town—you get home from work in a hurry."

The concern in his voice was real. Meg turned around and gave him a quivery smile. "That'll be fine," she said. "I'll unpack, and I'll sleep for a while. I'm really tired and grumpy."

She tossed the stuffed dog on the daybed and threw herself into her father's arms. "I love you, Dad."

"I love you, too."

Hugs were better than words, Meg decided, at least until they got used to each other again. Words got in the way—both the words they spoke and, of course, that everlasting, infuriating stream of words that came from his typewriter.

5

Meg woke the next morning with an unexpected feeling of well-being. Perhaps it was the dream she'd had just before waking—not one of the real dreams, but a pleasant vision of herself, her parents, and Bill walking down Brookfield Avenue together. Or perhaps it was the room Mrs. Larsen had given her. When she opened her eyes, the yellow walls and crisp curtains made it seem as if she were floating in sunshine.

She studied her new surroundings. On the wall opposite the bed was a photograph of a much younger Mrs. Larsen with a baby on her lap. They sat on the front steps of a house—this house—and Mrs. Larsen was smiling into the sun. A little to the left, and higher on the wall, was a narrow rectangle where something had once hung and had been taken away. The color in the rectangle was stronger than that of the surrounding wallpaper, as if it had been protected from the sun for a while.

There were other photographs next to the bed. In one, a much younger Caleb held a string of fish toward the camera. He was smiling proudly. In another, he sat in an armchair holding a tiny baby. He appeared to be twelve or thirteen in the second picture, and his expression had changed. It was sober and withdrawn, very much the look of the teenager who had met them on the porch yesterday afternoon.

Poor Caleb, Meg thought. She was ready to forgive his rudeness yesterday and his stubborn silence at the dinner table last night. She at least could visit her father; he had lost his father forever. She wondered how Mr. Larsen had died.

The thought of her father, right here in this house, made Meg jump out of bed in a hurry. They were going to have breakfast together! It was an unfamiliar house in a strange town, but when they sat down at the table, surely it would be a little like being one family again.

Mr. Korshak came out of his bedroom just as Meg reached the top of the stairs. He put an arm around her shoulder, and they went down together. "I suppose you still put peanut butter on your toast," he groaned as they entered the kitchen. "Disgusting habit."

Meg made a face at him. "And I bet you still put honey on your oatmeal."

Mrs. Larsen, busy at the stove, waved a good morning. "Some things never change," she said, clearly pleased to see the Korshaks smiling at each other. "No reason why they *should* change, I guess. The honey's on the table as usual, Jim, and the peanut butter's in the first cupboard on the right, Meg. Help yourself."

Minutes later, Steffi's elderly baby-sitter joined them. Meg liked Mrs. Tate. She and Steffi had kept the conversation lively at the dinner table last night, with no help from Caleb and only a little from Meg. Already Mrs. Tate seemed like a friend, her cotton-white hair pulled back in a neat knot, her thick glasses glittering in the sun.

Mrs. Larsen sat down with them and sipped coffee while they ate their cereal. Then she returned to the stove to fry one egg flipped over the way Meg's father liked it. Meg refused an egg, and Mrs. Tate's was served soft-boiled in an eggcup.

"You shouldn't wait on me, Kathy," Mrs. Tate said, but she looked pleased.

"Once a day won't spoil you," Mrs. Larsen replied briskly. "You do more cooking in this house than I do, I'm sure."

Meg enjoyed watching Mrs. Larsen move around the kitchen. She wore a flowered cotton dress today, as crisp and fresh as her uniform had been. She had a shining look, as if she were smiling, inwardly, all the time.

"Where's Steffi?" Meg asked when she'd eaten her second piece of toast. She wondered where Caleb was, too, but she was not going to ask about him.

"She's out in the backyard helping her big brother

weed the vegetable garden," Mrs. Larsen replied. "At least, Steffi calls it helping—that's not what Caleb calls it. In a few minutes she'll be in here complaining that Caleb is a mean brute who won't let her do anything."

Was that why Caleb was "catching it" yesterday? Meg wondered. No, that wouldn't fit the words she had overheard. ". . . quit moping about something you can't change." What was it that Caleb couldn't change? Meg reminded herself that it was none of her business, and she really didn't care. She had enough to think about without worrying about him.

Still, he was a boy, and he was good-looking. She and Rhoda spent hours talking about the boys at school—how to get their attention, how to talk to them once you had it. Even if she didn't say a word to Caleb all the time she was in Trevor—even if he didn't look in her direction once—she knew she'd tell Rhoda about him when she wrote.

"Now, how about that ride around town before I head for the typewriter?" Mr. Korshak asked. "Since we didn't get to it yesterday, I'll show you the highlights this morning, Meg."

Mrs. Larsen's smile flashed. "If you can find any."

"Oh, Kathy," Mrs. Tate said reproachfully, "there's our beautiful library, and there's the swimming pool and the band shell and the war memorial and—well, lots of places. Trevor is a lovely town."

"Of course it is," Mrs. Larsen agreed. "I was teasing. You two run along and see the sights. I'd suggest that you leave by the front door," she added, "unless you want Steffi tagging along to show you where all her kindergarten friends live."

In the blue sedan once more, Meg leaned back and stretched. Breakfast in a boarding house had turned out to be fun, and now she was alone with her father, as she'd wanted to be.

He smiled at her expression. "How's your mother, Meg? Do you think she's working too hard?"

Meg didn't know. "We fight a lot," she said softly. "Practically all the time."

Mr. Korshak pointed to the city library set in a neat square of lawn. It was small, but it was beautiful, as Mrs. Tate had insisted. "I don't like to hear that," he said. "You have to try harder, Meggie."

"I do try," Meg insisted. "It isn't my fault. Not always, anyway." She wondered if the tour of Trevor was going to be a time for scolding.

"You and your mother are so different," Mr. Korshak said thoughtfully. "About as different as two people can be, I guess. You're probably never going to think the same things are important, but that doesn't mean you can't learn to get along."

Meg wondered if that was true. Her mother didn't think winning the role of Princess Running Deer had mattered very much. If she knew about Meg's real dreams, she wouldn't think they were important either.

"You're just going to have to be tolerant," her father went on. "Give a little."

You didn't! Meg felt a rush of resentment. She remembered the evening before the morning her father had left them. The last argument had been over whether he should get a steady job or concentrate on his writing. Meg's mother had sounded shrill, even desperate, as she demanded that he find work. Neither of them had been tolerant of the other's concerns, and it had ended with her father moving out.

"Show me the swimming pool," Meg suggested, to change the subject. And after that they just looked at Trevor, avoiding serious conversation.

When they returned to the Larsens' house, a half hour later, Caleb was sitting on the front steps. He stood when the Korshaks came up the walk.

"You want to go to the bait shop with me?" he asked Meg gruffly. "It's a couple miles out of town."

"Good idea!" Mr. Korshak exclaimed, before Meg could answer. "You go along, Meggie, and I'll get to work." He gave her a quick kiss on the forehead and was up the steps before she could protest.

"You don't have to—" she began, feeling trapped.

Caleb stretched. "Suit yourself. I'm taking the pickup."

Reluctantly, she followed him around the side of the house. She was certain the invitation wasn't his own idea, and she was irritated with her father for pushing her into accepting. But she had nothing else to do, and if she refused now, Caleb might not ask again. *Hi, Rhoda,* a letter began in her head. *Caleb and I did an errand together this afternoon. We had fun.*

As it turned out, she never wrote that particular letter. . . .

6

The highway north out of Trevor twisted like a snake between dark forest walls. Caleb drove fast and well. He didn't speak to Meg until they rounded an especially sharp curve, and then he braked suddenly.

"Look!" His hand shot through the open window. "Deer."

For a moment Meg saw nothing but trees. Then a delicate tan shape moved out of the brush. Caleb slowed to a stop as the doe paused to study the truck.

"Fawn, too," Caleb whispered. A tiny spotted baby appeared behind the mother. For a moment the two people in the truck and the two wild creatures from the woods stared at each other. Then the doe led her baby out onto the highway. They crossed slowly, the mother's eyes always on the pickup, and vanished into the trees on the other side.

Meg had been holding her breath. Now she sighed

with delight. "That was just—just perfect. I've never seen anything so pretty."

Caleb gunned the motor. He looked pleased. "You were lucky," he said. "There are lots of deer around here, but I haven't seen a fawn for a long time."

"I'll never forget it," Meg assured him solemnly. She would have liked to thank him for inviting her along, but she didn't want to embarrass him. Maybe he guessed how she felt. The silence seemed more friendly now.

"Yeah, well, I guess that's something you can tell the kids back home," Caleb said after another mile or two. "City kids never see anything like that."

Meg didn't mind the touch of smugness. "I'm going to write to my best friend, Rhoda, tonight and tell her. I wish she'd been here."

"You can tell her about the bait shop, too," Caleb said.

Meg opened her mouth to say she didn't think Rhoda would find a bait shop particularly interesting —a store full of worms, for goodness' sake?—but then the truck hurtled around still another curve, and the words died in her throat. There, in a graveled clearing, was a gigantic fish. The curved belly rested on beams, and the tail rose higher than the surrounding pines. Wooden steps led to a gaping mouth where a door was set between jagged, gleaming teeth.

It was the fish of Meg's dream.

"Well, what do you think?" Caleb gestured at it with pride. "That's a musky, that is. Biggest game fish in the north. Not the kind of store you expected, I bet."

Meg cowered against the vinyl seat. *"That's* the bait shop?"

Caleb swung into the parking lot and maneuvered the truck into a space just in front of a sign that said JONES' FISHING SUPPLIES.

"The owner's name is Ray Jones, but everybody calls him Jonah." Caleb looked at Meg expectantly, then scowled. "It's a joke, see? Jonah. Big fish. What's the matter with you, anyway?"

"N-Nothing." She felt sick. The great fish loomed over the truck as if it were about to attack. Meg wanted to jump out and run, but she couldn't move. Her dream was beginning all over again, and this time she was awake.

"Come on in and look around, if you want to." Caleb continued to watch her curiously. "All I have to do is pick up some leeches."

"Leeches!" Meg almost choked on the word. "You're going to buy *leeches?*" A monster fish with its stomach full of leeches! She'd never seen one, but she thought she'd prefer an octopus.

"Best bait there is for walleyes," Caleb said briskly. He opened the door and jumped out. "Suit yourself whether you come in or wait here. What's the matter, is this too corny for a big-city girl?"

"Oh, no." He was annoyed because she couldn't, or wouldn't, admire the unusual bait shop. But how could she tell him the truth? He'd think she was crazy if she said she'd had a bad dream about a big fish and was afraid to go inside. "It's just this funny feeling I have," she said weakly. "I can't explain."

Caleb was disgusted. "What kind of funny feeling? You mean you don't like fish?"

"I guess . . . I don't know." Above her, the long white teeth of the make-believe musky gleamed. She stared up at them, trying to believe that the dread she'd felt in her dream had been caused by those wicked-looking fangs. But there was something else, and she knew it. She was afraid of what would happen inside. . . .

Caleb went up the wooden steps two at a time and disappeared through the mouth-door without a backward glance. Meg looked around her, trying to decide what to do. Maybe the bad thing was going to happen to Caleb! She'd let him go inside without a warning because she was afraid he'd think she was silly. He might be in trouble right now.

"Caleb, wait!" She jumped out of the pickup and ran up the steps to the porch that filled the front of the musky's mouth. Nothing to be afraid of here, but beyond the door the inside of the fish was dim and shadowed. She hesitated a moment, then threw open the door and plunged inside.

"Caleb!"

"Back here."

Not surprisingly, the interior was long and narrow. Gill-slit windows opened above racks of bright-colored fishing lures and displays of rods, reels, and bamboo poles. At the far end was a counter. Caleb was just picking up a round white carton.

Meg walked toward him, her heart pounding. She was terrified, even though the store seemed empty except for Caleb and the clerk behind the counter.

Caleb grinned at her. "Changed your mind, huh? Want to see what leeches look like?" He held out the carton.

The clerk's hand shot across the counter. "That'll be two dollars," he snapped. "Cash." He was a stocky, well-dressed boy of about seventeen. Meg looked at him in surprise and then at Caleb, whose face had turned a dull red. He reached into his pocket and slapped two dollar bills on the counter.

Meg turned toward the door. "I don't want to see leeches," she said. She was ready to run if Caleb insisted on opening the carton. "Come on," she begged. "Let's get out of here."

"Good idea." The clerk seemed to be agreeing with Meg, but he kept his eyes on Caleb. "I'm supposed to look after things here—and that includes keeping out troublemakers."

"What the heck is that supposed to mean?" Caleb demanded.

"It means I'm supposed to watch out for"—the clerk hesitated, as if realizing he might be going too far—"for shoplifters. Mr. Jones says I'm responsible—"

Caleb moved swiftly, and the clerk stumbled back against the wall behind him. One outstretched arm hit a rack of fishing rods and sent it crashing to the floor.

"Look at that!" the boy shouted. "If those rods are damaged, you'll have to pay for them!" His voice was shrill. "Of course, everybody knows you have the money—"

He stopped, silenced at last by the dangerous light in Caleb's eyes.

"Please, Caleb," Meg begged. "Let's go. Please!"

"Yeah, get out." The clerk snatched up one of the rods and held it in front of him. "Take your leeches and get out!"

Caleb scooped up the carton. "You can keep the leeches," he snarled. He ripped off the cover and turned the carton upside down. Instantly the floor was alive with black, writhing shapes. One of them landed on Meg's sneaker. With a scream that made her throat ache, she ran out of the bait shop, clattering down the wooden steps, two at a time. When she reached the truck, she was sobbing.

Heavier footsteps sounded behind her. Caleb slid into the driver's seat and started the motor. The truck roared out onto the highway.

Meg couldn't stop crying. The fear she'd felt from the first moment she saw the bait shop, the strange hostility between the two boys, and finally the sight of the leeches squirming on the floor had been too much. She didn't understand what had just happened, and she was too upset to care.

All she was sure of was that another dream had come true. Something bad had been waiting inside the giant fish.

A rustic sign appeared ahead of them: WAYSIDE REST STOP. Caleb slowed the truck and looked at his passenger. He was breathing hard.

"You want to mop up a little?" he asked gruffly. "You can't go home looking like that. I never saw anybody get hysterical over a few leeches before. They're no worse than night crawlers—with a sucker at one end."

"They're horrible," Meg sniffed. "Besides, it wasn't just the leeches."

Caleb turned off the highway and parked in a patch of shade. "What, then?"

"You know."

He leaned back. "You mean that business with the clerk?" he asked, as if the possibility had just occurred to him. "That was nothing, for pete's sake. Just a—a misunderstanding." He turned away to look out the window, and Meg realized he was waiting to see if she'd accept that explanation.

"What do you mean, a misunderstanding? You were mad enough to hit him! Not that I blame you," she added hastily. "He was calling us shoplifters."

"Me," Caleb said. "He was calling *me* a shoplifter. He never saw you before."

"Well, whatever. But you were buying the leeches, not stealing them. He acted like he wanted to make trouble." Meg's tears faded as she remembered the clerk's exact words. "He was terrible!" she exclaimed. "He acted as if—as if he *hated* you!"

"Maybe he does." Caleb's smile was a little scary. "I beat him in the ski tournament last winter—he didn't like that much. His name is Les Machen."

"But why did he call you a shoplifter?"

The smile disappeared. Tan fists clenched the steering wheel, and for a moment Meg thought he wasn't going to answer her question. Then he seemed to make up his mind. "Because he thinks my dad was a thief. Lots of people do."

Meg blinked. "Do what?"

"Think my father stole." Caleb gritted the words. "He worked at the Trevor Bank. Just before he was killed—in a car accident—a big chunk of money was taken from the bank. A lot of people in this dumb town think he took it. He and his best friend."

"But that's awful!" Meg exclaimed. "They shouldn't accuse him of a crime when he's dead and can't prove they're wrong." She looked at Caleb anxiously. "What about his friend? Did he tell people it wasn't true?"

"The friend was killed in the crash, too. That was nearly four years ago. Afterward, they found bank accounts in the friend's name in five or six different banks around the state. The money added up to exactly half of what was stolen." Caleb said the words fast, as if they tasted unpleasant. "The police never found the other half."

He started up the truck and drove back onto the highway, just as a fat porcupine waddled out of the woods. Meg was grateful for the distraction. She didn't know what to say next. Caleb's last words—*The police never found the other half*—hung in the air between them.

"Well, anyway," she said at last, "I'm sure your dad didn't steal the money."

Caleb slanted his eyes at her. "How would you know? You never met him."

"I just know," Meg said. "He wouldn't."

"No, he wouldn't." But there was something in the quiet way Caleb agreed with her that was more disturbing than anger.

"I meant it when I said I didn't blame you for hitting that clerk," Meg said. "That Les. I would have hit him if he'd said something mean about my father."

"He was saying it about me, as much as about my father," Caleb told her. "He thinks my mom and I have the rest of the money squirreled away somewhere. He thinks we'll start spending it in a few years when everyone's forgotten about the robbery. Half the town thinks so."

"No!" Meg protested. "You mustn't say that."

"Why mustn't I?" Caleb slowed the truck as they entered the town limits. "Hey, listen," he went on, "don't you say anything to my mom about what happened today."

"I won't."

"You'd better not! She's always on my case about 'forgetting the past and looking to the future' "—he parodied his mother's voice. "But she doesn't have to take the kind of garbage Les Machen and his buddies dish out. Maybe her pals at the hospital and the Historical Society make cracks behind her back, but they don't come right out and say her husband was a thief."

Meg remembered the words she'd overheard when she arrived at the Larsens' house: . . . *quit moping about something you can't change, for heaven's sake.*

"Maybe you'll find a way to prove he was innocent," Meg suggested. "That would be wonderful."

"And maybe I'll just get out of this darned town in another year," Caleb snapped. "That's what I really want."

Meg felt very sorry for him. Caleb was short-tempered and blunt, but he was deeply unhappy, too. "I wish I could help," she said. "Having people say bad things about your father must be about the worst thing in the world."

Caleb shook his head. "Not knowing is the worst thing. If I knew for sure what happened, I'd know what to do about it. Maybe my mom can live here without knowing, but I can't."

"You don't mean you think he did it!" Meg was shocked.

"I said he didn't do it. Period." He parked the truck in front of the house, and at once Steffi appeared on the porch, shouting a welcome.

"Remember," Caleb warned again. "Don't talk about any of this to the family."

Steffi raced down the walk and scrambled into the truck. Meg started to slide out from under, but suddenly Caleb grabbed her wrist and held it. "Hey, tell me one thing," he said. "What's the real reason you didn't want to go into the bait shop? I mean, nobody in her right mind would be afraid of a store because it was shaped like a fish, so why—"

Meg pulled her arm away. She would either have to lie and pretend she'd been afraid of the make-believe fish, or she'd have to tell the truth about her dream. Either way, Caleb was sure to laugh at her.

"Afraid of what?" Steffi demanded. "What are you afraid of, Meg? I'm not afraid of anything."

Meg's eyes met Caleb's. His bitter expression had faded as he waited for her answer. He wouldn't believe the truth. She remembered how hard it had been to tell Bill and Rhoda about the real dreams—and they were her brother and her best friend!

"I can't tell you," she said flatly and slid out of the cab. "Thanks for the ride, Caleb." She half walked, half ran to the house, followed by noisy protests from Steffi and total silence from Steffi's big brother.

7

Meg spent the next three days keeping out of Caleb's way. She went swimming in the town pool three times, twice with Steffi and once by herself. She wrote long letters to Rhoda, to Bill, and to Grandma Korshak, and she toured the town hospital with Mrs. Larsen as her guide. It was a quiet, pleasant enough time, but rather lonely, until she remembered the library. The Trevor Library was small and smelled faintly dusty, but its librarian was a friendly lady who encouraged Meg to wander through the stacks looking for old book-friends and new ones.

Weird! That's what Rhoda would say, if she knew that Meg was trying to avoid Caleb instead of getting to know him better. But Meg wasn't ready to talk to him again about her feelings at the bait shop. Caleb was moody and impatient—not at all like her brother, Bill. Even when he smiled, Meg sensed anger that bubbled and boiled just beneath the surface. She felt sorry for him, but she didn't feel comfortable with him. He made her think of a quiet-looking volcano that could send up showers of hot lava when you least expected it.

If she'd been able to spend more time with her father, maybe she wouldn't have cared so much if Caleb laughed at her. She was a stranger among strangers in Trevor, and she needed her father. He ought to understand that. But right after breakfast he went to his room, and for the rest of the morning the old manual typewriter clicked and clattered behind the closed door. At ten-thirty he appeared in the kitchen for coffee, and Meg was there waiting for him. At noon he took a half hour to relax after lunch, and they went for a walk or a ride. Steffi always begged to go along, but if Mrs. Larsen was at home she forbade it.

"Give Meg and her daddy some time alone together," she'd say, and they'd leave quickly, trying not to look back at the disappointed little person watching from the front porch.

Those brief times were the best part of Meg's day. She and her father talked mostly about Mr. Korshak's writing. Even though she continued to feel resentful, Meg began to understand why his work was so important to him.

"When I finish a story," he said one day, "I read it over, and maybe I think it's pretty good, but I can't be sure. What I *am* sure of is that I've done the best I can.

For the first time in my life I'm using whatever abilities I have. That's a great feeling."

He talked to Meg as if she were a grownup, and gradually her resentment faded. She was proud of what he was doing! Now, she thought, if only her mother were proud of him, too, they could forget the divorce and be together again. There was no good reason for her father to live in Trevor. He could write at home, if only her mother realized that he wasn't just wasting his time. Maybe if he explained it to her the way he'd explained it to Meg. . . . She braced herself to suggest it, but somehow their time together always ran out before she could find the words.

She looked forward to Saturday evening when Mr. Korshak wouldn't have to go to the newspaper office. Perhaps the two of them would go out for a hamburger feast, the way the whole family used to in the old days. But when Saturday finally came, Mrs. Larsen had her day off, too. Delicious smells wafted from the big kitchen, and Meg was invited to help carry bowls and platters from the kitchen to the dining-room table.

"Stuffed pork chops are my dad's favorite thing," she commented.

Mrs. Larsen's cheeks turned pink. "We all like them," she said quickly. "Caleb would eat pork chops five times a week if I'd let him."

As much as she had hoped for a whole evening alone

with her father, Meg had to admit that Saturday night dinner with the Larsens and their boarders was fun: Jeff Townsend, the traveling salesman, was back for the weekend, eager to tell about his adventures on the road. He was a young man, proud of his first job, and Meg thought it was nice the way Mrs. Larsen encouraged him to talk. She treated him like a second son. Old Mrs. Tate was practically a member of the family, too. Steffi called her Granny and chattered constantly unless reminded that she must give others a chance.

Caleb just ate and listened. Watching him, Meg thought of Bill, at home alone, probably eating a TV dinner at the kitchen table and reading while he ate. She decided she'd write to her brother again that night. She wanted to tell him her thoughts about getting her father to come home. Maybe if she and Bill both talked to their mother. . .

"If you want to go, say so," Caleb said impatiently. "It'll have to be dutch." Meg realized suddenly that he'd been speaking to her.

"Oh, Caleb!" Mrs. Larsen groaned. "What a way to ask for a date!"

Caleb shrugged. *"The Old Man and the Sea* is a fishing story—it's a classic movie, for pete's sake—and I want to see it. Since Meg is so crazy about fish, I thought she'd like to go along."

"Meg's crazy about fish?" Mr. Korshak looked puzzled. "I didn't know that. You and I'll have to go fishing while you're here, Meggie. I did quite a bit of it while I was living out at Uncle Henry's place."

Meg turned her back on Caleb, who was watching her with a suggestion of a grin. "I'd like that," she told her father. She would do anything that would give them time together.

"Well, what about it?" Caleb asked. "You want to see that big fish tonight?"

"I have a letter to—"

"Oh, Meg, don't be a wet blanket." Mr. Korshak spoke with unexpected sharpness. "Get out and have a little fun, for heaven's sake."

They were all looking at her now, wondering why she'd turn down the movie with Caleb in favor of sitting at home. She wanted to say, *He's just looking for a chance to ask questions about what happened at the bait shop.* But then Mrs. Larsen would want to know what *did* happen, and her father would want to know what kind of questions. She couldn't discuss her real dreams with them, either.

"You do what you want to do, Meg," Mrs. Larsen said. "It *is* a fine film, though. I remember seeing it years ago."

"I'll go with you, Caleb," Steffi offered. "I love movies."

"No, you won't," Caleb retorted. "The last time I took you, you talked through the whole picture."

"I'd go myself," Mrs. Tate said brightly. "If a handsome young man asked me, I'd say yes in a minute!"

Meg was beaten and she knew it. "Okay," she said. "I'll go. As long as it's dutch."

They left right after the lemon meringue pie—another of her father's favorite foods. Mrs. Larsen wouldn't even let Meg help to clear the table. "Just run along and have fun," she ordered. "There's plenty of help for the asking around here."

The theater was on Lakeview Avenue. The ride downtown had been a silent one, and Meg welcomed the excitement of the tourist-filled main street. "It's like two different towns," she commented, and immediately regretted breaking the stillness.

Caleb looked bored. "Don't they have crowds in Milwaukee?"

When they'd found a parking place and started down the street toward the theater, Meg put as much distance as possible between them. Occasionally she paused in front of a store window, pretending to see something of interest. Caleb made no attempt to stay close to her. It was not until they reached the theater ticket office that they came together again—just as Les Machen walked out of the lobby with three other boys.

Meg's stomach lurched. *Don't let him start again,* she prayed. Without thinking, she moved between Caleb and his enemy. Maybe Caleb was sarcastic and difficult, but he had a reason for being the way he was. Les

Machen was just mean. Meg could tell he enjoyed hurting people, and she despised him for it.

The boys passed without speaking. When they were gone, Caleb grinned down at Meg, a friendly, open smile. "Regular tiger, aren't you?" he commented. "You looked like you were ready to punch the guy."

"I was," Meg said. She was trembling.

All through the film—which was very good, even if it was about a fish—Meg kept recalling Caleb's smile and what he had said. Could they be friends after all? He'd sounded as if he was pleased that she'd been ready to fight Les Machen; at least, he didn't resent her wanting to help. Maybe he needed a friend to count on as much as she did.

There was one way to find out. *I'll tell him about the fish dream,* she decided. *I'll show him that I trust him.* Having made up her mind, she settled back to enjoy the film, wishing Rhoda could see her now.

"You mean you were scared to go into the bait shop because of a dream?" They were sitting in the Pixie Drive-In parking lot. Caleb took a long drink of his Coke and watched Meg over the rim of the cardboard cup.

She nodded. It had been hard to say the words, and already she knew she'd made a mistake. "My grandma says the dreams are like secret windows. To look into the future. I guess you think that's crazy."

Caleb leaned back. "You've got a good imagination,

that's all. Maybe because your dad is a writer. Maybe you're going to be a writer, too—when you grow up."

When you grow up! Meg felt tigerish again, only this time it was Caleb she wanted to attack. Why had she thought they could be friends? He was laughing at her. He considered her a silly little kid who made up things.

"It's not my imagination, Caleb Larsen," she snapped. "I really knew something scary was going to happen inside that fish. I knew it, and I don't care whether you believe me or not. It's happened to me lots of times before. I even have a dream book—"

"A what?"

"A dream book. When I have a real dream—that's what I call them—I write it down just the way I remember it. Then I wait to see if it comes true."

Caleb finished his drink and pitched the cup into a nearby wastebasket. "Did you write down the dream about the big fish?"

"Of course I did. Even though I didn't see how that one could come true. I mean, I didn't think there could be a fish that huge anywhere." She glared at him defiantly. "But there was."

"Show me the book."

"No!" The only people who had seen the dream book were Bill and Rhoda. It had felt safe and right to share this unexplainable part of her life with them, but they were special. "You'll just make fun of it."

"Well, then . . ." Caleb's mocking smile returned.

"Forget it," he said. "So you had a bad dream—lots of people have 'em. No big deal." He started the truck and reached for her milkshake container. "You through with that?"

Meg nodded. "My dreams *do* come true sometimes," she said angrily. "I really don't care whether you believe me or not."

The drive home was as silent as the earlier one had been. "Thanks for taking me to the movie," Meg said coldly, when they turned into the driveway. "I liked it."

"No big deal," Caleb repeated. "You paid your own way."

"Well, thanks for the milkshake then."

She crossed the yard to the house, and when Caleb didn't follow, she continued on inside by herself. A light was burning in the dining room, and she peeked in to see Mrs. Tate playing cards with Steffi. From out on the front porch came voices—her father and Mrs. Larsen, talking quietly in the dark.

It occurred to Meg that they must have seen the truck turn into the driveway, but their conversation continued without a break. The murmuring voices made Meg feel shut out. After all, she'd just had her first date. Sort of. At least, it was the first evening she'd spent with a boy who wasn't her brother. It would be nice if somebody asked if she'd had a good time—even though the answer would have to be no.

"Three's company," the mocking whisper was right

behind her, "in case you were thinking of going out on the porch."

Meg whirled to face Caleb. "Don't be silly!" she retorted. "I can talk to my dad any time I want."

"Can you?" He sounded mocking. "Well, don't say I didn't warn you. Why do you think the old folks were so anxious to get us out of the house? They wanted to be alone."

For the second time that evening Meg longed to hit him. "That's stupid!" she exclaimed, forgetting to keep her voice down. "That's the stupidest thing I ever heard of."

Caleb stepped around her and started up the stairs. "No, it's not. That's the straight stuff, dream girl," he said calmly. "Mrs. Tate keeps Steffi busy with a deck of cards, and Caleb takes Meg to the movies. Don't look so upset. I don't mind baby-sitting once in a while."

8

Meg lay very still, as if by not moving she might sink like a stone into sleep. But she was still wide awake when her father came upstairs, opened her door a crack, and then tiptoed away. Twenty minutes later she heard Mrs. Larsen climb the stairs and stop to look in at Steffi before going to her own room. The house settled into a darkness that was gentler and quieter than the city-dark at home.

It was strange, Meg thought, how she could lie as still as a statue, and at the same time her thoughts could swarm and buzz like a hive of furious bees. She hated Caleb now—really hated him—and it wasn't because he had called their date a baby-sitting job. She hated him for the terrible thing he'd said about their parents. It couldn't be true. She wouldn't believe it. Someday her father and mother were going to be together again. Surely her father hoped for that, too, even if he pretended to like living in Trevor.

She considered getting up and tiptoeing into his room to remind him of all the wonderful times they'd had on Brookfield Avenue. Caleb was crazy if he thought her father would forget those days, just because someone made his favorite stuffed pork chops and lemon meringue pie every Saturday night. A thousand great dinners wouldn't make a person forget his real family.

She didn't get up. Her body felt as if it were made of lead, and besides, she wasn't sure she was ready to confront her father with what Caleb had hinted at. Maybe it would be better to call Bill and ask him what to do. She tried to imagine what her brother would say. Probably he'd tell her to calm down until she had some proof.

If only she could go back to the way things had been before this evening! She felt as if the Meg who had ridden north on the bus was a very different person from the Meg lying here in the dark. All that other Meg had wanted from this summer was a chance to be Princess Running Deer and do pleasant, ordinary things with her best friend when they weren't appearing in the play. It could have been a wonderful vacation. Now it was a horrible one. What was worse, it would continue to be horrible even after she returned to Milwaukee, because then she wouldn't know what might be happening here in Trevor.

The thought of her mother, who didn't know Mrs.

Larsen existed, twisted Meg's stomach in knots. If what Caleb suggested was true, her mother would be heartbroken, wouldn't she? Meg realized she didn't know how her mother would react. Mrs. Korshak had wanted the divorce, but surely she must think, at least once in a while, of how wonderful it would be if they were all together again.

The grandfather's clock in the downstairs hall struck twelve before Meg drifted, at last, into an uneasy sleep.

The dream that followed wasn't one of her real dreams, but she remembered it clearly when she awoke the next morning because it was so strange. *Another dream about a big fish!* She rubbed her aching head. For a girl who'd never caught a fish in her life—or wanted to—she was giving a lot of thought to the subject.

She sat up, feeling grubby and wrinkled in the clothes she'd worn the night before. She hadn't even undressed, hadn't done anything but lie on her bed and hate Caleb. Now she took a quick shower and dressed in fresh jeans and a halter top. Glittering sunlight made her a little less uneasy. After all, Caleb liked to tease. Maybe he had decided to scare her last night because she'd refused to show him her dream book. Well, whatever his reason, she didn't want to talk to him ever again. She wasn't going to listen to any more of his stupid ideas about her father and his mother.

He was waiting at the foot of the stairs. "Listen," he whispered, "don't get the wrong idea about what I said last night."

Meg bit her lip. She waited for him to move out of her way.

"I mean, when I said that stuff about baby-sitting —nobody asked me to take you to the movie. I was just in a lousy mood when I said that."

Meg felt a rush of relief so overwhelming that she forgot her decision not to talk to him. "Then it wasn't true!" she exclaimed. "What you said about my father and your mother wanting to be alone."

Caleb didn't answer right away. Out in the kitchen, Mrs. Larsen was singing softly to herself as she worked. Upstairs, Steffi called to Granny Tate. "I don't know about all that," he said, at last. "It's none of my business anyway. I just didn't want you to think they told me to invite you to the movie. That was my own idea."

He turned away, looking so uncomfortable that Meg panicked all over again. "But it's not true, is it? *Is it?*"

Caleb opened the front door and went out on the porch, motioning Meg to follow. He settled in the big swing and waited until she sat, reluctantly, beside him.

"What the heck is so wrong if our folks like each other?" he demanded in a low voice. "It happens."

"But my dad already has a family." Meg felt ready to

explode. "He already has a wife in Milwaukee."

"Not anymore," Caleb said. "He doesn't have a wife anymore, and having kids isn't going to stop him from getting married again if he wants to. People do it all the time."

Married! "He doesn't want to," Meg said, close to tears. Faced with Caleb's blunt comments, she didn't know how to argue.

"Hey, don't you like my mom?" he asked curiously. "I think your dad's okay. He's probably going to be famous someday, and we'll all be glad to be related to him." He cocked his head at her and grinned.

Meg turned away. If she didn't, she was afraid Caleb would see how close she was to crying. He would never understand how disturbed she was by his talk of marriage. Liking or disliking his mother had nothing to do with it. Meg would have felt the same about any woman threatening to take her mother's place.

"Anyway," Caleb went on, "I'm through with school next year, and then I'm going to get out of this town so fast you won't believe it. My mom is going to need somebody—"

"To run errands and take out the garbage," Meg said bitterly.

"Sure," Caleb agreed. "And to keep her company. She gets pretty depressed sometimes, even if she pretends everything is great. I can tell."

"Well, it doesn't have to be my father who keeps her

company," Meg said. She jumped up and started toward the front door. "I don't want to talk about it any more, do you mind?"

"I don't mind." Caleb was right behind her. "Hey, tell me more about your dreams that come true."

"No! You don't believe me."

"Sure I do. I'm sorry I teased you. I told you, I was just in a lousy mood last night."

Meg wished he would go away, but talking about dreams was better than talking about Mrs. Larsen needing a companion. "Well, I had another dream about a fish last night," she offered cautiously. "But it wasn't one of the real ones."

Caleb's eyebrows shot up. "Another big fish?"

"I saw a man and a little boy fishing," she said slowly. "All of a sudden, this fish jumped out of the water, right near the boat. I don't mean a big one like the bait-shop fish. It was three or four feet long, but it had those same sharp teeth and really mean-looking eyes. It kept circling the boat on the end of the man's line, and when it got up close, the little boy began to cry."

Caleb had started to open the front door. Now he stopped and leaned against it. "So then what happened?"

"The man was yelling at the little boy. He kept shouting, 'Get the net! Get the net!' And the little boy picked up a knife from the bottom of the boat and leaned out over the edge. He was going to cut the line because he was afraid of those horrible teeth, but the man yelled some more and jerked the line away. I don't know what happened after that—guess I woke up."

Caleb looked stunned. "I'll tell you what happened after that," he said. "The man caught the fish and took it home and had it mounted to hang on the wall. It was a record-sized musky. Meg, that really happened to me! I was six years old, and I almost made my dad lose the biggest musky of the season—" He stopped. "What did he look like—the man in your dream?"

Meg tried to remember. "He was tall and thin and —and he had a young face, but his hair was all gray."

"That was my dad!" Caleb was practically shouting now. "His hair turned gray when he was just a kid. Listen, Meg, that's a really terrific trick you have there!"

"It's not a trick," Meg protested. She was thoroughly confused by what Caleb was saying. "It wasn't even one of the real dreams."

"Because it's not *going* to happen," Caleb said, as if he'd never had a doubt in the world about real dreams. "It's *already* happened. To me! I wonder what it means. It has to be important, Meg—your dreaming about something that happened to me a long time ago."

"Meg! Caleb! Breakfast." Mrs. Larsen's cheery call from the kitchen saved Meg from having to reply. She was sorry now that she'd told Caleb this latest dream.

He didn't understand that most of her dreams were just . . . dreams. Looking at his excited expression, she knew she'd have a hard time convincing him that this particular dream was just a coincidence.

"It's crazy," Caleb marveled. "I never heard anything like it. You've got to let me see your dream book, Meg. I mean it. I want to look at the book myself."

Meg sighed. "Okay," she said. "Okay, then." Her father was coming downstairs, and hearing his footsteps reminded her of what was really important.

She'd let Caleb read the dream book. What difference did it make, anyway? If her father was going to marry again, she didn't care who read the book. She didn't care about anything.

9

Dear Princess Running Deer,

    I hope you're having a terrific time to make up for not being in the play. The Princess we have—Yellow-Hair got the part—isn't much. Every time she says her big farewell speech, I think about how much better it would sound if you were doing it. Mr. Cody does, too, I can tell. He gets this funny look on his face, like he's wishing he'd signed up for softball coaching this summer instead of theater-on-wheels.

    Actually, being in the play is fun, but it would be a lot more fun if you were in it, too. Instead, you're off there in the north woods having dates with Handsome Boys. And who knows what other exciting stuff! Oh, speaking of Handsome Boys, Bill came downstairs after supper last night, and we sat on the front steps for a long time, just the way you and I always do. I guess he thought I was lonesome, which I was.

My dad is working extra hours this week, and I'm usually asleep before he gets home.

It was the third time Meg had read Rhoda's letter. She liked picturing her brother and her friend sitting on the apartment steps, telling each other what had happened that day. Rhoda thought Bill was perfect—that was another wonderful thing about Rhoda. She considered him the smartest and nicest boy in Milwaukee, and Meg agreed.

If only they could all be there together on the steps for an hour or so, Meg knew she'd feel better. There was so much that needed telling. She'd tell them that ever since she'd shown Caleb the dream book, he'd been watching her with something close to awe, as if he expected her to pull a rabbit out of a hat or walk on air. More important, she'd tell them that during the last few days she'd been watching closely for signs that her father and Mrs. Larsen cared about each other. She was convinced now that it was true.

They smile at each other when they think no one's looking. If Mrs. Larsen doesn't have to work in the evening, they sit on the porch and talk after everyone else has gone to bed. He bought her a present yesterday—a map of Wisconsin the way it looked a hundred years ago. We've had lemon meringue pie twice in four days. . . .

"Meg, do you want cold fried chicken or ham sandwiches or both in your lunch box?" Mrs. Larsen's sudden appearance on the porch made Meg jump, as if her thoughts might be easily read. The trouble was that she couldn't hate Mrs. Larsen, even if she wanted to. Caleb's mother was warm and cheerful and unfailingly kind. She obviously liked Meg and wanted her to enjoy her time in Trevor.

"Both, I guess, My father—"

"—has a healthy appetite. It's going to be even healthier when you two are out on a lake breathing all that fresh air." Mrs. Larsen nodded at the giant post-card lying next to Rhoda's letter on the swing. "You've heard from your mother, haven't you? Is she having a good time in New York?"

"Oh, yes." Meg held up the card so Mrs. Larsen could see the picture of the Central Park Children's Zoo. "She and my uncle Bill went up in the Statue of Liberty and to the top of the World Trade Center, and they ate at Rockefeller Center, and she bought me a bathing suit and a book at Bloomingdale's." It was a book on acting. Meg knew that was her mother's way of saying she was sorry Meg had missed her chance to be Princess Running Deer. It was a pretty special gift, since Mrs. Korshak almost certainly thought acting in a play wasn't very important. Just as she thought writing stories and novels wasn't important.

"Well, I'm glad she's having fun." Mrs. Larsen sounded as if she meant it. "I'll be leaving for the hospital in a couple of minutes, Meg, and Caleb has already gone on a round of errands. I've asked Granny Tate to take Steffi to the drive-in for a hamburger—

otherwise she'd make a terrible fuss about going along with you. When your dad finishes his writing for the day, you'll find your lunch box in the refrigerator."

"Thanks, Mrs. Larsen."

"You have a wonderful time, now."

"We will." Meg tried to match the landlady's tone, but it wasn't easy. She'd been alternately looking forward to and dreading this afternoon ever since her father had suggested, a couple of days ago, that they go fishing together if he could get time off at the office. They would rent a boat, take their lunch, and have a whole afternoon to themselves. A week ago Meg would have been thrilled, but now she wasn't at all sure she wanted to spend hours alone with her father. Maybe he'd suggested the outing because he had something to tell her. Something he knew she wouldn't want to hear.

When Mr. Korshak came downstairs, just before twelve, he didn't look like a man with a serious announcement on his mind. "What a beautiful day!" he exclaimed. "You ready to go, Meggie?" He pushed his old narrow-brimmed hat well back on his head. "I've promised Kathy we'll bring home fish for dinner tonight."

Kathy. Mrs. Larsen. "I'm ready," Meg said. "But don't count on me for a dinner. I don't know anything about fishing."

"Don't know a whole lot myself," her father replied. "Not like some of the natives around here who know the lake bottom better than their own backyards. Just the same, I caught my share when I was living out at Uncle Henry's place."

They gathered fishing rods and the lunch box, and Meg checked to make sure she had her brand-new license in the pocket of her jeans. The bait was in a cottage cheese carton—three dozen night crawlers that Caleb and her father had dug the evening before while Meg held the flashlight. She was grateful that her father hadn't suggested using leeches. She still shuddered every time she remembered the squirming black shapes on the bait-shop floor.

"We'll make a fisher-person out of you yet," her father promised as they headed out of town in the blue sedan. "By golly, I've been looking forward to this!" He hummed softly and glanced at Meg as if he hoped she'd join in.

"How did your writing go today?" Meg asked. The question sounded stiff and formal, but she couldn't help it.

"It's going beautifully, Miss Sobersides." Her father reached over and pulled her long braid, just the way Bill always did. "My book is going well, and so is everything else. Now relax and enjoy yourself."

"I guess Mom is having a good time, too," Meg said. "I got a postcard from her this morning."

"Glad to hear it." He pointed up the road at a sign bearing the profile of an Indian and an arrow. "Indianhead Lake," he said. "That's where we're going. Carpenter's Landing is at the end of the road, and they have boats and motors for rent."

He swung into a narrow lane that wound under low-hanging branches. Meg took off her sunglasses. She didn't want to miss seeing a deer if one poked its head out of the brush.

A small log cabin stood in the clearing at the end of the road, and beyond it a half-dozen boats bobbed in the sparkling water. "You go on down to the shore and pick out a boat," her father said. "I'll check in at the cabin and find out where the weedbeds are."

Obediently, Meg picked up the lunch box and one of the fishing rods and made her way to a narrow pier. The air was sweet, and the clear brown water rippled in the breeze. *Weedbeds,* she thought. Was fishing really all her father had on his mind? She wanted to think so, but she doubted it. *Get it over with,* she ordered herself sternly. *Ask him.* But how do you ask a question like that?

Her father jogged down to the shore, his fishing rod over his shoulder, and stepped lightly into the boat she'd chosen.

"The best weedbed's straight across the lake," he reported. "There's a little bay, and right at the mouth of it—" He broke off. "What's the matter, Meggie? Not seasick before we start, are you?"

"I'm okay," Meg said. "Why do we want to find a weedbed?"

"Because that's where fish find *their* dinners, dear girl. Mrs. Carpenter says she and her husband go over there two or three times a week and catch all they can eat."

He adjusted the motor, tugged the starter rope, and brought the boat roaring to life. Meg was impressed; he handled the boat as if he'd been doing it all his life. At first she faced forward, hoping the cool cut of the wind would help to whisk away her worries, but as they neared the other shore she turned to face her father. He smiled at her, and she realized with a pang that he was a handsome man. She'd never thought of that before, but it was true. And he had a kind look, much like Bill's. *Of course Mrs. Larsen is in love with him,* she thought despairingly. *Why wouldn't she be?*

It was an afternoon Meg wouldn't forget. Her father taught her to bait her own hook, chuckling when she squealed at the cool slipperiness of the worms and cheering loudly when she landed her first perch after just two minutes of watching the bobber dance on the water. There was a fish basket—a wire cage with a hinged cover—that dangled in the water, and this was where the fish were put as soon as they were caught.

At the end of forty-five minutes there were six fish in the basket, and Meg was beginning to relax. They had talked about nothing but fish, the beauty of the shoreline, and whether Meg was setting her hook quickly enough after the bobber dipped under water.

"It's time we took a lunch break," Mr. Korshak decided. "Wash your hands over the side of the boat, and we'll see what Kathy fixed for us."

"What about the fish in the basket?" Meg asked. "How long can they stay cooped up in there?"

Her father shrugged. "They're fine. At this point they probably don't even know they're in trouble."

Meg felt a pang of sympathy for their catch. Their fate was already settled, and still they swam around in the underwater basket without a care. *That's how I was until this week. Just going along, thinking there was a chance our family would be together someday—and all the time it was too late. Maybe.*

"Kathy packs a terrific picnic lunch, doesn't she? . . . Don't you love it out here on the water? . . . I want to spend the rest of my life close to a lake. . . ." Even though he didn't come right out with an announcement, it was easy to read meanings into every word her father said. As they were finishing their lunch and packing away cups and scrap paper in the hamper, he asked ever so casually, "How do you like the Larsens, Meggie? Aren't they a great family? You know, Kathy has been through a bad time without letting it beat her. She's one of the most remarkable women I've ever met."

"I like her," Meg said honestly, and waited for what would come next. Her father looked very sober, and for a moment he returned her stare. Then he grinned and stretched. "Time for us to get back to work, I guess. We've got a lot of fish to catch if we're going to provide dinner tonight."

Meg discovered she'd been holding her breath. He wasn't going to tell her now. She was going to be left like the perch in the fish basket, not knowing what lay ahead. Poor fish. Poor Meg.

"You're looking glum again, Meggie. What's the matter, does fishing bore you?"

Her father sounded so concerned that Meg forced a smile. "I'm not bored at all," she said. "I guess I was beginning to feel sorry for the fish."

Mr. Korshak laughed. "Don't think about it," he advised. "Concentrate on how good they're going to taste with fried potatoes and coleslaw."

"And lemon meringue pie?" Meg couldn't resist.

"Maybe," he agreed. "We can hope."

Meg threw out her line. Suddenly she was remembering how her father had left the apartment on Brookfield Avenue, early one morning, two years ago, without saying goodbye to his children. He hated scenes, so he'd simply walked away while they were still in bed, assuming that she and Bill would understand. Maybe, she thought, after she returned to Milwaukee, a letter would arrive one day announcing that her father and Mrs. Larsen were married. He had taken the easy way once; he would probably do it again.

The bobber danced and turned on the ripples without dipping below the surface. After a while Mr. Korshak moved the boat farther down the shore, and then to a different weedbed, but it was no use. The fish had stopped biting.

"It's probably your fault, Meg," he teased. "You can't start feeling sorry for the darned things. They know it, and it scares them off."

"What'll we do?"

"Try for another half hour and then call it a day. It's after four anyway."

Meg was astonished. She felt as if she'd been in a trance ever since lunch, her thoughts turning and drifting like the bobber, pulling her in a hundred different directions. She was tired, tired, *tired* of her family's problems. She was tired, too, of being the one who was left behind. Her mother went to New York, Bill went to college, and her father was secretly planning a whole new life for himself. It wasn't fair.

Caleb has the right idea, she thought. *I'm going to leave home the very day I finish high school. I'll get a job in California or in New York City, or maybe in Hawaii, and I won't write to anyone unless they write to me first.* Just thinking about getting away made her feel a little better. Later, she decided, she might marry and have six children, and if that happened, she'd never, never leave them. . . . Or maybe she wouldn't get married at all! If you didn't get married and you didn't have children, you could do what you wanted without hurting anybody else.

"Actually," her father said, "I think you're ready to stop right now, aren't you?"

Meg glanced at him. For one startled moment she was sure he was reading her thoughts. Then she realized he was talking about fishing.

"I guess so. But if you want to stay a while longer, it's okay with me."

"I think they're through biting for the day." He leaned over and swung the fish basket into the boat. The captured fish leaped and slapped against the wires. "What'll we do with these?" he asked. "It's up to you, Meg."

"What do you mean, it's up to me?"

"I mean we can take these home and clean them and freeze them until we get some more—or we can let them go. By the time they're cleaned, six little perch won't make a meal for six hungry people tonight."

Meg came out of her trance. "Let them go!" she exclaimed. "Oh, let them go!"

He opened the basket and emptied the contents into the lake. Six streaks of silver shot away into the cool darkness.

Her father watched Meg's expression with amusement. "By golly, you *did* feel sorry for them," he said. "Maybe you're going to be a vegetarian."

"I don't think so," Meg said. "That's not why I wanted to let them go."

There was no way she could explain why she felt better now that the basket was empty. She could hardly explain it to herself.

10

She stands just inside a neatly trimmed hedge and watches Steffi and her best friend, Astrid, climb the steps of an old house. The house looks as if it has recently been painted; the grass is cut to a smooth carpet. But all the window shades are drawn, and to Meg, watching the children but unable to move or call to them, there is something disturbing about the stillness of the place.

Steffi tries the front door, then moves to the windows that open on the porch. She and Astrid take turns trying to open the nearest window. It sticks at first, then slides up, and the children crawl through the opening.

Now Meg is inside the house. She stands in a dim front hall and calls Steffi's name. There is no answer. The girls must be beyond one of the two closed doors opening off the hall, or perhaps they have run up the wide stairway straight ahead. Meg opens the right-hand door and steps into almost-dark. Behind her, the door closes soundlessly. The only light comes through the narrow spaces around the drawn shades.

Meg stands very still, suddenly aware that there are dozens—no, hundreds of eyes peering at her from the dark. They are all around her and above her, too. At first she's too frightened to move. The eyes seem to draw closer. Then she looks down and screams. She's standing toe to toe with two monstrous hairy feet. They are huge, clawed and evil-looking.

She leaps backward, hitting her head against the closed door. Frantically she fumbles for the doorknob, finds it at last. She rushes out into the hall and slams the door behind her, whimpering with terror. When she turns around, a tall, thin, gray-haired man is watching her. He says nothing, but he opens the door across the hall and gestures to her to go through it with him.

I'd rather die! Meg thinks.

And wakes up.

Coming back from a real dream was like stepping into a theater lobby after an exciting film. Meg looked at the flowered paper on her bedroom walls, the curtains hanging limp in the sunlight, the picture Steffi had made for her and taped to the bureau mirror. She touched her face with exploring fingers and rubbed her eyes as if she could rub away the pictures of the last few minutes. It was impossible.

That's the worst part, not being able to say, "Oh, well, it's just a dream." She knew it was more than that.

Tomorrow or the next day or some day after that, this dream would come true.

The sheet was twisted around her legs. Meg kicked her way free and found her dream book in its hiding place under her T-shirts in the bottom bureau drawer. There was a ballpoint pen clipped to the cover. She crawled back into bed and began to write a description of the dream while all the details were fresh in her mind.

The old house . . . the children disappearing inside . . . the eyes staring at her from the darkness. The huge, hairy feet almost touching her own! This was more than a dream; it was a nightmare. And the worst part had been the ending. The tall, thin, gray-haired man in the hall had been a terrible shock, partly because Meg hadn't expected anyone to be there, and partly because he'd looked at her with such a strange, pleading expression. She shuddered, remembering how he'd opened the door on the opposite wall and motioned her into gaping blackness. The thought that all of this was actually going to happen again—that this time she might be forced to pass through that open door—frightened her badly.

She had to get up, move around. After tucking the dream book safely back in its drawer, Meg pulled on yellow shorts and a yellow shirt with SAVE THE WHALES lettered across the front. Then she tiptoed down the hall to see if Steffi was safe in her bed. *I wish*

Rhoda was here, she thought. *If Steffi's gone and I have to go looking for her right now—if the dream is going to start coming true this minute—I just don't think I can stand it all alone!*

She opened Steffi's door a crack and peeked in. The little girl slept soundly in a nest of Raggedy Ann-printed sheets. Her favorite teddy bear, wearing a baby bonnet and a blue diaper, was cradled in one arm.

Meg tiptoed back down the hall to the bathroom. She was trembling with relief. *I'm not going to let Steffi out of my sight all day,* she decided. *If I stay close to her, maybe I can keep the dream from happening.*

At the top of the stairs she hesitated. Someone was talking downstairs. The voice was low, and at first she didn't recognize it. Then she realized it was Mrs. Larsen who was speaking. She sounded sad and angry.

Meg knew she shouldn't eavesdrop, but she couldn't make herself move. Mrs. Larsen was always cheerful! Not since that first day, when she'd scolded Caleb for moping, had she ever sounded troubled or unhappy.

"—can't believe a son of mine would do such a thing! Fighting . . . breaking things . . . whatever got into you?"

There was a pause, and then Caleb said something. He sounded angry, too.

Mrs. Larsen cut his reply short. "I really don't care what Les Machen said. That's not the point. It's what *you* say and do that I care about. People can always make life miserable for you if you let them, Caleb. But you don't have to let them! I've told you that a hundred times."

There was a longer silence. Meg held her breath. She could imagine Caleb, his handsome face sullen, rejecting every word his mother said.

"Don't you think I hear my share of that kind of nasty talk?" Mrs. Larsen asked, and now her tone was more gentle. "Les's mother is one of the worst, but there are others. Every time I buy a new dress, I wonder if people are saying, 'Look at her—she's starting to spend the bank money her husband stashed away.' When we bought the pickup, Mrs. Machen actually told me she wouldn't have thought it possible that we could afford two cars. You have to ignore that kind of talk, dear. Laugh it off. You have to!"

Caleb muttered something that sounded like "—no use."

"Now don't say that!" His mother was cross again. "You're going to have to apologize to Mr. Jones for what happened in his bait shop. He wouldn't have called me if he wasn't very upset. And if there was any damage done, you'll have to pay for it yourself. I'm not going to cover the cost when you can't control your temper."

The screen door slammed, and heavy footsteps thudded down the back steps. Meg darted into the bathroom. *Poor Caleb,* she thought. Les Machen must have made it sound as if what happened at the store had been entirely Caleb's fault. Not that she blamed Mr. Jones for being disgusted if he came back to find the floor littered with those horrible leeches! Still, he should have waited to hear Caleb's side of the story before complaining to Mrs. Larsen. It was easy to see why Caleb could hardly wait to leave Trevor behind him.

When she went downstairs, Mrs. Larsen was in the kitchen making a sandwich for her lunch. Caleb was gone.

"Good morning, Meg. You look as if you picked up some more tan yesterday, even if you didn't bring home any fish."

"I guess I'm not much of a fisher-person," Meg admitted. "But I loved being out on the lake. It was really peaceful."

"It's that, all right." Mrs. Larsen's smile was warm. "It would do us all some good to take a day like that every couple of weeks. Enjoying the outdoors helps a person remember what's really important."

Meg went to the cupboard and began taking out dishes.

"Just set places for you and your dad and Granny Tate and Steffi," Mrs. Larsen told her. "Caleb ate earlier—with me." Her smile faded briefly, then returned. "We had things to talk about, and breakfast seemed like a good time to get them out of the way." She wrapped her sandwich in waxed paper and tucked it into a neat plaid lunch box. "As long as you enjoyed the lake so much, why don't you ask Caleb to take you fishing again sometime soon? He loves to fish, and he ought to do it more often. He forgets how lucky he is to live in this part of the country."

Meg brought cereal and milk to the table and slipped bread into the four-slice toaster. She didn't answer because she didn't know what to say. A girl didn't just tell a boy she wanted to be taken on a fishing trip—at least, Meg didn't. Mrs. Larsen ought to know that. But suddenly Meg was eager to talk to Caleb for a different reason. If she described the old house in her dream, maybe he could tell her where it was and what weird and terrifying things went on there. He would certainly be interested in the tall, thin man with the young face and gray hair.

"Where's Caleb now?"

"Out in the garden doing some weeding before it gets too hot." Mrs. Larsen looked wary. "He *might* be a little grumpy this early in the morning, dear, but just pretend not to notice. If he's owly, he'll get over it. You go ahead and talk to him about a fishing trip, and I'll call you when the others come down for breakfast."

The backyard was long and narrow and smelled of sweetpeas and freshly cut grass. Meg stood in the shade of the maple tree, where Steffi and Astrid usually played house, and looked down the path to the garden. There was something distinctly unfriendly about the set of Caleb's shoulders as he moved back and forth among the neat green rows. His back was to the house, but even at this distance Meg could see that his neck was an angry red.

She started down the walk, clearing her throat a couple of times to let him know she was there.

"Hi, Caleb."

"Hi." It was close to a growl.

Meg hesitated at the edge of the garden. She was probably foolish even to try to talk to him about her dream right now. Yet he'd been tremendously excited about her last dream—the one he'd decided was about himself and his dad—and he'd wanted to read the dream book. Hearing about the old house and the gray-haired man might take his mind off Les Machen and Mr. Jones for a while.

"I had another dream last night," she started uncertainly. "A real one."

Caleb leaned on the hoe in an elaborate pantomime of patience. "So?"

"So I thought . . . Well, if you don't want to hear it—"

"I don't!" The pretense of patience vanished. "I just want to be by myself, okay? I wish people would stop nagging me!"

Nagging? Meg retreated rapidly. She couldn't go back to the kitchen; Mrs. Larsen would guess that Caleb had been rude, and the scolding would start all over again. She scurried around the side of the house, climbed the porch steps, and threw herself into the big swing.

The vinyl cushion cooled her burning cheeks. Nagging! Caleb made her feel as if she were five years old and the worst pest in the world.

Everyone has a bad day once in a while. That was what Rhoda would say if she were here, but then, Rhoda was careful never to expect too much from anybody. Meg pushed the forgiving words out of her mind and hit the cushion with her fist.

She ought to go right back out there and punch him. He didn't have any right to blame his troubles on her. He had a wicked temper and his manners were terrible and—

—and he has a lot on his mind, Meggie. How would you feel if people kept hinting that you were a thief?

Meg stopped hitting the cushion. *Okay, okay,* she answered the Rhoda-voice. *But I'm still mad at him.*

Meg sighed and stood up. Rhoda had to understand that Caleb might look like a storybook hero, but he acted like—like a little kid. He could be very nice, and he could be prickly as a porcupine. He was complicated!

Like everyone else, Rhoda said, having the last word, as usual.

11

"You should have taken me with you," Steffi said. "I know how to catch fish."

"I bet you do." Mr. Korshak patted the little girl's hand. "Next time we'll take you along. You see, Meg and I haven't been together much for a long time, so we had lots of things to talk about."

"What things?"

"Oh, a whole list," Mr. Korshak said vaguely. "You're a good girl not to make a fuss."

Steffi, who had obviously planned to make a fuss, looked confused. Meg ate her cereal and listened to the conversation with interest. It made her more certain than ever that her father had expected to use their time on the lake to tell her he was going to marry Mrs. Larsen. He'd lost his nerve at the last minute, but that was what he had planned.

"I wanted to go," Steffi insisted.

Mr. Korshak looked at Meg. "Just think how much

Astrid would have missed you," she offered. "Besides, you'd have been bored, Steffi. We sat in the boat for hours and hours."

"I wouldn't have minded. I like sitting." Steffi slid out of her chair and headed toward the back door. "Astrid and I are going to play house," she announced. "You can play with us if you want to, Meg."

"Steffi, wait a minute." Meg tried to sound casual and failed. "Did Mrs. Tate say you could go outside before she came downstairs?"

"She has a headache," Steffi reported. "It's a *very* bad one. She said we could play in the backyard till she gets up, and then we'll go for a walk with our babies."

Meg sat back, aware that her father was watching her curiously. "Don't worry about Steffi, Meg," he advised. "She's an independent little thing."

Meg had no good reason to insist that Steffi play indoors, especially if Caleb was still working in the garden. She promised herself that as soon as her father went upstairs to write, she'd go out on the porch where she could watch the little girls every minute.

If only she could talk to her father about that dream! But he wouldn't want to hear about it, she knew that. *You make life more difficult than it already is,* he'd told her once. *A good imagination can scare you to death if you let it.*

"That's another thing about living in a small town," he said now, complacently. "Kids are safe in Trevor."

Maybe, Meg thought. *Maybe not.* She wished her

father good luck with his writing and busied herself washing dishes and wiping the vinyl table cover. Then she gathered up a mystery book, a box of stationery, and a pen, and hurried out to the back porch.

Astrid had already arrived. The children had carried cartons from the garage, and these were arranged under the maple tree, serving as cupboards, cradles, and cars. Caleb was gone, and so was the pickup.

Meg settled on the top step and opened the box of stationery. She'd write to Rhoda first, and then to Bill. She couldn't write to her mother because she didn't have an address. By this time she and Uncle Bill would have left New York City and would be in Pittsburgh visiting the rest of the family. Probably their mother called Meg's brother regularly, counting on him to relay news and greetings.

> *. . . wish you were here—you and Bill. Trevor's a pretty town and the Larsens are nice people, but, boy, do I miss you! I've had this really scary dream, and I can't talk to anybody here about it. And—this is weird—Caleb's dad, who's been dead for years, keeps showing up in my dreams. Crazy, huh? . . . And besides all that, I have a feeling that my dad and Mrs. Larsen—*

She crumpled the letter into a tight ball. It was no use; writing down her fears and suspicions was too painful. She'd have to wait till she got home to share what was happening in Trevor. For now, a quick note would have to do, with just a hint of the many important things there would be to talk about when they were together again.

She'd finished Rhoda's letter and begun one to Bill when Mrs. Tate appeared at the back door. She was very pale, but she said she felt a little better, and she thanked Meg for keeping an eye on Steffi.

"We'll go for a long walk after lunch," Mrs. Tate said. "I'll be fine by then."

But at lunchtime she was lying down again, this time on a couch in the living room. Caleb returned, and he and Meg took sandwich makings from the refrigerator and poured glasses of milk. They didn't speak. Meg wondered if his still-sullen expression meant that he'd driven out to the bait shop to apologize to Mr. Jones.

At twelve-thirty, Mr. Korshak came downstairs. He looked glum, too, and Meg guessed that the writing had not gone smoothly that morning. *What a cheerful group we are!* she thought— Caleb like a thundercloud, Granny Tate still pale and miserable, and her father's mind obviously on his work upstairs.

Only Steffi was her usual bubbling self. "When we play house, I'm the mama and Astrid is the grandma," she said. No father, Meg noted. Steffi couldn't remember what it was like to have one, and Astrid's parents were divorced.

"Caleb, will you build us a tree house this afternoon? It wouldn't take long." Steffi eyed her big brother, seeming to sense that this might be the wrong time to ask a favor.

"Can't," Caleb answered gruffly. "I have to cut grass at Millers' all afternoon. And trim bushes. And weed their garden." He sounded abused.

"But that's wonderful, Caleb!" Granny Tate exclaimed. "You've been wanting some jobs like that, haven't you?"

Caleb looked embarrassed. "Sure," he admitted. "Don't mind me. Bad day. Again."

Mr. Korshak stood up. "We all have them," he said. "I'm off to the newspaper office. I promised to work some extra hours to make up for yesterday. See you all tonight." He gave Meg a quick peck on the forehead and tousled Steffi's silky blond hair as he left. Caleb followed him out the door almost at once.

"You lie down," Meg told Mrs. Tate. "I don't have anything to do but watch Steffi. I'll sit outside and read."

The old lady looked grateful. "I haven't had a headache like this in years," she said. "Maybe if I rest just a little while longer..."

With Steffi's help, Meg quickly cleared the table and washed the few dishes. Then they went back outside. Astrid appeared almost at once, and Meg settled on the steps once more with her mystery book.

She must have dozed. The next thing she knew, the

telephone was ringing and her book was lying on the bottom step. Steffi and Astrid were looking at her and giggling.

"Meg, telephone," Mrs. Tate called. "It's your brother, I think."

Meg's first reaction was joy, followed almost immediately by panic. Why would Bill call in the middle of the day? He was supposed to be at work.

The sound of her brother's voice, surprisingly deep for such a beanpole of a boy, reassured her. "How's everything there, kiddo? Are you and Dad having a great time together?"

"We're fine." She couldn't tell him the truth, not with Mrs. Tate lingering close by, looking anxious. "What's wrong?"

He didn't answer her question. "I had a call from Mom last night. She and Uncle Bill are with the family in Pittsburgh. She sent her love to you—hoped you were having fun."

"I'll be glad when she gets back. Have you seen Rhoda?"

"Every day. She's mostly busy with the play." There was a long pause, and Meg held her breath. "The thing I called about...," he continued carefully, "Grandma Korshak is sick. She's in the hospital."

"The hospital!" Meg clutched the phone, and Mrs. Tate gave a little gasp. "What's the matter with her?"

"Don't know. They're doing tests. She had a dizzy spell in her apartment yesterday, and the lady who

lives downstairs called the paramedics. It may be
nothing serious. . . ." His voice trailed off, and Meg
knew he was as worried as she was. Nothing must
happen to Grandma Korshak. They loved her and
needed her so much.

"When will you hear about the tests?" Meg's voice
trembled.

"Tomorrow, maybe. I took the morning off and
went to the hospital. Grandma's cheerful, the way she
always is, but I think she's kind of scared, too. I talked
to her doctor, and he said they'd know more in
twenty-four hours."

It sounded like forever. "Dad's at work," Meg said.
"I guess you can call him there."

"No need. I won't have anything else to report till
tomorrow. Just tell him what I said, okay?"

"Okay."

"And try not to worry, kiddo. Grandma said she
didn't want us to worry, and she definitely didn't want
anybody coming home because of her. Got that? She
even scolded me for taking the morning off."

"Right."

"And one more thing. Grandma said to tell you she
had a dream about you. She can't be feeling *too* bad or
she wouldn't be talking about a dream, would she?
She said you were wearing a yellow dress, and you
looked like a princess—those are her words, not
mine."

"I don't even have a yellow dress." Meg knew Bill

was trying to cheer her before hanging up, but she couldn't respond.

"Well, then, you'd better run right out and buy one. If it'll make Meg Korshak look like a princess..." When she didn't laugh, Bill gave up. "Try not to worry, kiddo. I'll call again as soon as I know something."

Meg said goodbye and turned forlornly to Mrs. Tate. "My grandma's sick," she said, and burst into tears.

Mrs. Tate put her arms around Meg's shoulders and hugged her. "Come along, dear," she said. "A cup of tea will help. At least, it's always helped my generation. News is seldom as bad as it seems at first, and tea helps you to see more clearly." She was chattering, filling up the silence.

Meg wiped her eyes with the back of her hand. *Nothing's as bad as it seems at first,* she repeated to herself. *It mustn't be!*

She couldn't lose Grandma Korshak. Not now. Not ever. All through the divorce, and before, when Meg's parents were arguing constantly, Grandma had been the steady, serene presence they relied on. Meg felt especially close to her, since Grandma, too, had real dreams. She'd helped Meg accept the fact that she was different from most people.

Hesitantly, Meg began to talk, telling Mrs. Tate what a wonderful person her grandmother was. "She's my friend," she said, sipping her tea. "The way you're Steffi's friend."

She set the cup down, hard, in its saucer. Steffi! During the last few minutes Meg hadn't given her a thought. She was sure Granny Tate had forgotten about her, too.

Meg jumped up and ran to the back door. The cradle boxes, cupboard boxes and car boxes were scattered around the lawn under the maple tree. The little girls were gone.

12

"Now, Meg, there's no need to get in a state." Mrs. Tate stared at Meg in astonishment. "You've gone all white, dear. Come back and finish your tea. The children just got tired of waiting for their walk, I'm sure. They've decided to go by themselves. They'll take their dolls around the block and be back before you know it."

"No, I have to find them! Right away!" Meg dashed across the porch and down the steps. "Don't worry, Mrs. Tate!"

"I'm *not* worried, dear." Mrs. Tate followed her out on the porch. "They shouldn't have gone alone, but there's no need to fuss. Children are perfectly safe in Trevor."

Meg raced around the side of the house and looked up and down the street. A little boy was riding his tricycle near the end of the block, but there was no sign of Steffi and Astrid.

Meg didn't even know where to start looking. The old house in her dream was like dozens of other houses in Trevor, though she couldn't remember seeing one exactly like it. *Gray,* she thought. *It was gray, freshly painted. The bushes across the front looked as if they'd just been trimmed.* Maybe there was a house like that on the next street. If Caleb hadn't been so rude this morning, she would have described it to him, and he probably would have recognized it. Surely the house was close by; otherwise the children wouldn't go there by themselves.

Meg ran back along the side of the house, through the garden, and between towering sunflowers that separated the Larsens' yard from the neighbor's behind them. Steffi and Astrid weren't on the next street either. The only gray house was a tiny bungalow banked with pink geraniums.

Meg raced to the corner, feeling as if she were caught up in a waking nightmare. Her sneakers felt like iron boots, and she knew she might be running in the wrong direction entirely. *Trevor!* she thought. *Trevor is one awful place!* Steffi was gone, and Grandma Korshak—she tore her thoughts away from what might be happening to Grandma. She must find Steffi and Astrid before she thought about anything else. The little girls mustn't face the horror that had stared at Meg from the darkness in her dreams. Steffi mustn't confront a ghost—the ghost of her own father—by herself.

On the next block some boys were playing ball in the middle of the street. Meg wondered if it were possible that the children had walked this far. She started toward the ballplayers to ask if they'd seen two little girls, and then, as she ran, she caught a glimpse of tall gray gables at the end of the block. Her stomach lurched with the suspicion that she might have found what she was searching for.

She had. The house, set well back from the street, dozed in the sun, with its window shades closed like sleeping eyes. Meg forced herself up the concrete walk to where two tiny doll buggies stood side by side. She examined the house. It was hard to understand why the girls would have picked this place to enter. It looked deserted.

"Steffi? Astrid? Are you in there?"

The window next to the door was half open, its shade limp and unmoving. Meg glanced over her shoulder, longing for someone to tell her what to do. She *could* go home, ask Mrs. Tate where Caleb was working, call him, and . . . But there was no time to do all that. If Steffi and Astrid were in danger, they needed her now. She'd have to look for them alone, just as she had in the dream.

She climbed the steps and crossed the porch to the open window. With a last look at the street behind her—so safe, so ordinary looking—she lifted the shade and stepped over the sill.

The entrance hall was the way she'd seen it in her

dream—shadowy and dim, a closed door on either side, a flight of stairs straight ahead. There was a smell of fresh paint and of floor wax.

"Steffi, can you hear me?" Meg waited, willing the little girls to answer. Then she crossed the hall to the door on her right and opened it a crack. It was the hardest thing she'd ever done. This was where the really terrifying part of the dream had begun.

"Steffi?" She stepped into the room, holding the door open behind her. Hulking shapes loomed ahead and on every side. Eyes glittered in the dark, just as they had in her dream. The *things,* whatever they were, filled this room on either side and hovered overhead.

Hardly breathing, Meg waited for her eyes to grow accustomed to the dark. Gradually she was able to identify one shape, then another. A deer and its fawn stared at her from one corner. Across from them, a wide-antlered buck lowered his head to fight off two coyotes. Porcupines, foxes, woodchucks, and a badger were posed around the room. A mother wolf and her pups wrestled in front of a fireplace. Overhead, an eagle soared near the ceiling, and owls glared solemnly from branches attached to the walls.

Stuffed animals! The door started to slip from Meg's grasp, and she leaped to stop it. Even if the animals weren't real, she didn't want to be alone in the dark with all those staring eyes. She didn't want to see— she looked down and squealed with fright. The terrible clawed feet were there, practically touching her sneakers. When she looked up, she saw that she was standing under the outstretched forepaws of a black bear.

For a second Meg couldn't move. She knew the bear wasn't alive, but as she stood there, frozen, the great furry arms seemed about to swoop down and crush her.

"No!" The sound of her own voice broke the spell. Her feet, which until then had seemed glued to the floor, moved of their own accord, carrying her in one leap through the doorway and out into the hall. There she stopped, caught up in a new terror. The gray-haired man—the ghost-man who was surely Caleb's father—would appear now and try to coax her through the doorway on the left.

But the hall was empty. She leaned against the wall, her head whirling. The heat and the heavy smell of paint made her sickish, and her eyes ached as she strained to see into one corner and then another. At any moment the gray-haired man might appear in those shadows. Ghosts did that, coming and going as they wished. She looked longingly at the front door, but Steffi and Astrid were still here in this strange house. She couldn't leave without them.

"Steffi?" Her voice quivered. "Steffi, where *are* you?"

She would have to search. They could be anywhere, and if every room of the house was as frightening as the first one she'd entered, she didn't think she could stand it. At least, she thought, she could leave the room on the left for last. That was the one the ghost had wanted her to enter, and it was just a few steps away. Surely if Steffi and Astrid were in there, they would have heard her by now and called to her.

Unless they're tied up and gagged and helpless. Unless they're unconscious. Unless they are . . .

The uncarpeted staircase curved upward into gloom. Meg mounted the first step and then the second, pausing after each to listen for a creaking floorboard overhead or a childish voice calling for help. Each time she stopped, the silence closed around her like a blanket.

On the fifth step Meg stumbled and almost fell. She would have slipped all the way to the bottom if she hadn't caught the banister and hung on. Jolting pain, as one knee hit the edge of a step, pushed her over into panic. She burst into tears.

"Steffi!" she screamed. "Steffi, where are you?"

As if in answer, behind and below her the door on the left burst open. A shriek cut through the stillness, and before Meg could turn around, something hit her hard between the shoulder blades.

13

They stood hand in hand at the foot of the stairs, their laughter fading rapidly as they looked up at Meg.

"We fooled you, didn't we?" Steffi sounded uncertain. "It was funny, wasn't it? We hid when we saw you coming up the walk." She picked up her teddy bear and straightened the bonnet that had almost slipped off when he was thrown. "Teddy wanted to scare you, so we let him do it," she said with a sidewise glance at Astrid.

Astrid shifted from one pink-sanddled foot to the other. "Naughty old teddy," she added. "He's really naughty, isn't he, Meg?"

Meg collapsed on a step and buried her face in her hands for a moment. When she looked up, the little girls were watching her, wide-eyed.

"Teddy isn't naughty," she said unsteadily. "You are! Both of you! You think it's funny to scare a person half to death, but it isn't. It's mean and cruel! You ought to be ashamed of yourselves."

Steffi's face puckered. "I don't see why you were *so* scared, anyway," she whined. *"We* weren't scared. The museum is a very good place. It's like a school. My mama said so."

"Museum?" Meg looked around, her anger set aside, briefly. "This is a museum?" She thought of the only museum she knew, in Milwaukee, a vast, modern building that housed hundreds of exciting displays.

"Sure. But it's not finished." Steffi was relieved at this change of subject. "My mama's helping to clean it up and paint it and stuff. I came with her and helped once."

A museum. Of course. That explained a room full of stuffed animals.

"What's in there?" Meg demanded, pointing at the door on the left.

Steffi shrugged. "Just—nothing important. I like the animals better. And the people upstairs."

Meg jumped up so fast she almost lost her balance again. "What people upstairs?"

"Not real people, Meg." Astrid giggled. "They're like big dolls, and they're wearing old-timey dresses and funny hats. Steffi showed me." She looked fondly at her friend.

"I'll show you, too, Meg," Steffi offered.

Meg shook her head. It was annoying to think of the little girls enjoying a leisurely tour of the museum while she raced from one street to another, trying to find them so she could save them from—whatever. "I don't want you to show me anything," she said coldly. "I've already seen the animals, and that was enough. Besides"—the thought occurred to her for the first time—"if the museum isn't open to the public yet, we aren't supposed to be in here. We could be in big trouble. Your mama's going to be so mad—"

"She won't care," Steffi said. But she looked scared.

"Oh, yes, she will. Wait till she finds out you opened a window and sneaked in when no one else was here."

"Let's not tell her."

Meg was sick of the whole conversation. The most frightening dream of her life had just come true, or most of it had, and she knew she'd never forget the experience. The gray-haired man had failed to appear, but the children's "joke" had been just as terrifying. She didn't want to talk about any of it.

She herded the children to the open window and raised the shade so they could scramble out onto the porch. As soon as she was alone, the heavy silence settled around her again, and now she had an uncomfortable feeling that she was being watched. At the far side of the hall, under the stairs, one shadow seemed darker than the rest. It was tall, thin . . . With a little moan she climbed through the window and slammed it shut behind her.

Steffi and Astrid were tucking their babies into the

carriages for the journey home. "Let's go," Meg ordered. "Come on, hurry!"

She set off down the walk at a rapid pace, and after a moment the children followed. No one spoke again until they reached the corner, and then Steffi touched Meg's hand timidly.

"Do we have to go so fast?" she asked. "The sidewalk's all bumpy and Teddy doesn't like it."

"Granny Tate is probably worried sick about you." Meg didn't care how crabby she sounded. "The sooner we get home, the better."

When they reached the Larsen house, Astrid announced her legs were tired from all that fast walking and she was going home. Steffi parked her doll carriage at the foot of the front steps and watched her friend scurry away.

"Are you going to tell Mama where we were?" The blue eyes were unhappy.

"I haven't decided." Meg wanted to make sure Steffi understood the seriousness of what she'd done. "You might have caused a lot of damage in the museum, you know. Or someone besides me might have seen you there and had you arrested!"

"Arrested!"

"Sure, arrested. You can't go breaking into places any time you feel like it."

The screen door opened, and Mrs. Tate came out on the porch.

"Well, there you are!" she exclaimed, but she looked only at Steffi. "You had your friend Meg very upset, dear. You really shouldn't wander off like that. Has Astrid gone home?"

Steffi nodded, still overcome by her close escape from the law.

"I hope you didn't cross any streets by yourself," Mrs. Tate continued. "Did you?"

Steffi glanced quickly at Meg, then nodded again.

"Well, that was naughty of you." The old lady bent and gave Steffi a quick hug. "I think you'd better stay indoors the rest of the afternoon. We'll play some games if you like."

Left alone on the porch, Meg realized she'd hurt Mrs. Tate's feelings by rushing off to look for the children. She threw herself into the big swing and glared out at the street. What a day this had been! There was the bad news about Grandma Korshak, and then the nightmare-dream had mostly come true, and now practically everyone was annoyed with her or had hurt feelings.

Except for her dad and Mrs. Larsen, of course. They were just thinking about each other.

—*If you want to feel sorry for yourself, I'll play some sad music.* That was what Rhoda would say if she were here. But for once the thought of her best friend didn't make Meg feel any better. "It *is* a bad day!" she muttered aloud, and gave the swing such a push that she bumped her knees on the porch railing.

* * *

Her father came home at six and called Bill at once to see if he'd heard anything more from Grandma's doctors. Watching him on the phone, Meg realized he was terribly worried. She wanted to go to him and put her arms around him while he talked to Bill, but instead she just sat, slumped, in an oversized chair, and watched. After a while Mrs. Larsen tiptoed down the hall from the kitchen and laid a hand lightly on his arm. She left it there only a moment, but Mr. Korshak glanced up from the phone and seemed comforted.

"Bill will call tomorrow," he said when he'd hung up. "We'll just have to wait, I guess."

What else? Meg thought grumpily. Waiting was one thing she'd remember about Trevor. Waiting for her father to say he was going to marry again. Waiting to find out the meaning of the real dream that had partly come true. Waiting to hear whether Grandma Korshak was going to be all right. She got up and stalked out of the room, almost bumping into Caleb in the hall. He grabbed her arm as she started to pass him. "Hey, about this morning . . ."

Meg glared at him.

"I guess I was sort of—uh—"

"Yes, you were."

Caleb looked pained but determined. "You said something about a dream. Was it one of the special ones—the kind in your dream book?"

"If you really want to know, it's already come true—at least, part of it has."

"No kidding!" Caleb exclaimed. "Tell me about it."

Meg hesitated. After the way he'd acted this morning, Caleb didn't deserve her confidence. But the dream, unlike most of the real dreams, was still a mystery, since it hadn't entirely come true. She wanted to forget it, but the thought of the gray-haired man wouldn't go away. Why would Caleb's father—if it *was* the ghost of Caleb's father—appear once again? It was possible that Caleb might be able to guess the reason. There was no one else she could talk to about it.

There was an outraged exclamation from the kitchen. "No! You did *what,* young lady? Are you serious?"

A small, quivering voice replied.

"Don't tell me you didn't do anything wrong." Mrs. Larsen sounded angrier than Meg had ever heard her. "You had no business going into the museum without me. I never would have taken you there in the first place if I'd thought you'd go back by yourself. You go up to your room this minute, and stay there till I say you can come down."

Steffi hurtled through the hall, past Meg and Caleb, and up the stairs.

"What's the big rush?" Caleb called after her.

The little girl whirled at the top of the stairs and

stuck out her tongue at Meg. "I thought *she* was going to tell, so I told first!" she shouted, as if that explained everything. Her bedroom door slammed behind her.

"Meg." Mrs. Larsen appeared at the kitchen door. "May I speak to you for a minute?"

She waited, arms folded, for Meg to join her. Caleb trailed along behind.

"Steffi tells me she and Astrid broke into the museum this afternoon, and you found them and brought them home. I can't imagine what got into her to do such a thing, but I'm grateful to you for finding her. Do you think they did any damage?"

"I didn't stay long enough to find out," Meg admitted. "I don't think so, though. Steffi just wanted to show Astrid the exhibits—"

Mrs. Larsen brushed away the explanation. "Really, I'm sick about this. If she did break something, I'll never hear the end of it. As if there isn't enough talk about the Larsens in this town!"

So that was it. Caleb was wrong if he thought his mother wasn't troubled by gossip. Meg felt a rush of sympathy for Mrs. Larsen, who kept so much to herself.

"Want me to go over there and check things out, Ma?" Caleb asked.

The lines in his mother's forehead softened. "That's a good idea," she said. "I still have the key we used when we were painting—it's in my bureau upstairs.

Just take a quick look around, and be sure to lock the window they used to get in." She started toward the hall, then paused. "Meg, how in the world did you know where to look for the children? The museum is three blocks away."

Meg studied a bouquet of snapdragons on the table. "I—I just ran around till I saw the kids' doll buggies," she said. "And then I saw the open window."

"Well, thank goodness you got there before anyone else noticed," Mrs. Larsen said. "I'm more thankful for that than I can say."

Meg squirmed. She didn't want to lie to Mrs. Larsen, but she certainly hadn't told the whole truth. She realized that Caleb was watching her with interest. When his mother had gone upstairs to Steffi, he grinned knowingly.

"That was the dream, huh? You dreamed the kids went to the museum by themselves, and when they disappeared you knew where to look."

The grin was infuriating. "I never even knew there was a museum," Meg said. "I *might* have known, if you had let me tell you about the dream this morning."

Caleb shrugged. "Oh, well, this way you got to play detective, right? Maybe you can go into business —a one-woman lost-and-found department."

Meg narrowed her eyes. *Boys!* she thought. *Smart-alec, know-it-all boys!* Well, she knew how to make this one take her seriously.

"There was a man in the dream, too," she said casually. "He was tall and thin and gray-haired. It was the same man I dreamed about before."

The know-it-all grin disappeared like magic.

14

"He just stood there looking at me," Meg said for the third time. Now that she'd finally described the dream to Caleb, he couldn't seem to hear it often enough.

"Are you sure he didn't say anything?"

"I've told you and told you—he just stood there. He seemed kind of—kind of sad, I guess. And I could tell he wanted me to go into that other room."

She took running steps to keep up with Caleb's long strides.

"It has to mean something," Caleb said, "my father showing up in your dream like that. Don't you think so? Maybe he'll be there in the hall when we go in."

His intensity frightened Meg. So did the thought of walking in on Mr. Larsen in the museum's front hall. "The whole thing is so mixed up," she complained. "I mean, I've *never* dreamed about a ghost before. Maybe it isn't your father—"

Caleb didn't seem to hear. "What I think is this. I

think you have a special *thing* that lets you pick up on stuff other people miss. It lets you see into the future —a secret window, you said your grandma called it. So maybe this time there's a ghost in the window."

The explanation was scary, but it was no more frightening than the rest of this day had been. Only a couple of hours ago, Meg had promised herself never to go near the Trevor museum—or even think about it—again. But once she'd told Caleb the dream, there was no way she could avoid going with him. She'd become a kind of connection between him and his father. He'd begged her to come with him, making it sound like the most important thing in the world.

Maybe it wouldn't be so bad this time. After all, she had someone with her, and she knew now that the staring eyes and clawed feet in the dream belonged to harmless stuffed animals. Still, when she and Caleb reached the museum and turned up the walk, she couldn't help hanging back. The house looked forbidding in the moonlight.

"Spooky," Caleb commented when they reached the porch. He switched on his flashlight and pointed the beam at the front door. "I used to be afraid of ghosts when I was a little kid. I pretended to look forward to Halloween because everybody else did, but I really hated it. I'll tell you something, though, Meg—it's different when the ghost you're looking for is your own father."

Meg couldn't imagine what that would be like.

"The ghost part of the dream might not come true," she warned. "We don't know—"

"Don't try to take it back now, Meg." Caleb was determined. "That was my father you saw. I know it!" He swung the flashlight across the shaded windows. "I hope he *is* here. I want to see him and ask him . . ." His voice cracked as he started up the porch steps. Meg followed. She thought of her own father, who was alive and close by. *Even if he gets married,* she realized, *we can still be together sometimes. I'll still have him.*

Caleb unlocked the front door and they slipped into the hall.

"Shine the flashlight over here," Meg whispered. "There must be a light switch."

"No way," Caleb replied. "If we turn on lights, someone in the neighborhood will notice, and they'll call the police. We'll do our looking around with the flashlight."

He found the window the children had used to enter and fastened the latch securely. "Okay, that's done. Now, where did you see my—the man in the dream?"

Meg gestured toward the closed door on the left. "He was right there. And Steffi and Astrid hid in that room this afternoon when they saw me coming."

Caleb played the light over the door, around the hallway, and up the stairs, while Meg held her breath. "Do you see anything? Is he—"

Pity for Caleb, together with her own nervousness, made Meg irritable. "I don't see anything," she retorted. "Let's check the displays the way your mother asked us to and get out of here. Please, Caleb!"

"Right." Caleb focused the light on the door on the left. "We'll start in there."

Meg groaned. She wanted to say she'd wait for him in the hall, but that would mean being alone in the dark. Reluctantly she joined him as he opened the left-hand door.

The flashlight revealed a long room divided into aisles by three display cases. Caleb directed the beam of light into the nearest case. It held dozens of fish, neatly mounted in rows, with identifying cards below them. The second case contained lake maps and drawings of underwater scenes, and the third was full of spears, carved fish lures, and different kinds of reels.

"I remember my mom talking about a Lakes Room," Caleb said. "This must be it." He moved the light over the walls. "But why would my dad want you to come in here? Sure, he liked to fish, but I don't see—"

Meg took the flashlight from his hand and passed the beam more slowly over the displays and into the far corners of the room.

"What is it? Do you see something?"

She couldn't explain her sudden certainty that someone, or something, was in the room with them. If she put the thought into words, she knew she'd panic and run.

"Come on, Meg, tell me what you're looking for.

Or give me back the flashlight and we'll go search another room."

The invisible presence became so real that Meg was astonished that she was the only one to sense it. It was as real to her as was Caleb, who had seized her wrist and was switching the light impatiently back and forth across the room. The beam picked up a display of turtles on a side table, a painting of fishermen caught in a storm, another painting of Indians fishing with spears like the ones in the display case.

"Caleb, I'm scared—" The beam of light swung sharply upward, and Meg gasped in protest. "Why did you do that? You're hurting my arm."

"I didn't do anything," Caleb snapped. "I'm trying to find the darned door."

His voice came from the other end of the room.

Meg opened her mouth to scream, but no scream came out. She tried to run, but her legs wouldn't carry her. She couldn't move her wrist, held in fingers of iron that she had thought were Caleb's. All she could do was stand there, struggling to breathe, and stare up at the wall where the flashlight beam rested.

It revealed a huge, beautifully mounted fish.

"Hey!" Caleb sounded excited. "You know what that is?" He hurried on, not waiting for an answer. "That's the record-sized musky my dad caught when I was six years old. It's the fish he caught the day—" He hesitated.

Never mind all that, Meg begged silently. *Help me,*

Caleb! Something's holding my arm! Help me!

"Meg, that's the fish my dad caught the day I tried to cut the line. You know, it happened in the first dream you told me about!"

Meg's knees threatened to give way. This was worse than any dream she'd ever had. With a tremendous effort she turned her head and saw darkness—a towering darkness, deeper than that of the rest of the room. As she stared, the darkness thinned. The pressure on her wrist relaxed, and she almost dropped the flashlight.

"Hey!" Caleb bumped into the display cases as he made his way back to her. "Keep that light up there on the fish. This could be important, Meg." She heard him come close, felt him seize the flashlight from her numb fingers. The beam swung back to the giant musky.

"Isn't he a beauty? When my mom fixed up the sewing room, she packed the fish away, and then when the town started planning a museum, she told me she was going to donate it. I forgot all about that till now. She said my dad was a terrific fisherman, and she wanted Trevor to remember something good about him. I'm glad you found it up there."

Meg clung to the display case. She was trembling violently. "I—I didn't," she whispered. "I mean—"

Caleb was caught up in the discovery of the musky. "My mom was right," he went on with satisfaction. "It looks great."

Meg rubbed her wrist. She could still feel the pressure of those invisible fingers. She had better think about something else—anything!—or she'd run out of this room and never stop running.

Images from her first dream about the fish and then the second flashed through her mind. What was the connection? She had dreamed first about the catching of the fish. Then in the second dream Caleb's father had appeared and tried to coax her into the Lakes Room. Now he had returned while she was wide awake, and had directed the flashlight toward the musky. . . .

"What's the reason?" Meg wondered out loud. "Why is that fish so important, Caleb? I think your dad—I think he wanted us to see it up there."

For a moment, she and Caleb stood side by side, staring upward.

"I'll need something to stand on," Caleb said suddenly. "Come on."

They went back to the entrance hall, and after a short search they found a stool tucked in the open space under the stairs.

"This'll do. You carry the flashlight, Meg, but keep it low. We don't want anyone else charging in here now."

It took all of Meg's courage to return to the Lakes Room. "You can hold the stool steady or you can tremble like that," Caleb muttered. "Not both. What is the matter with you, anyway?" Without waiting for an answer, he climbed up on the stool and reached for the fish.

It looked heavy, but to Meg's surprise he lifted it off the wall with one hand and lowered it to her easily. "All the taxidermist uses is the skin, the head, and the fins," he explained as he scrambled down from the stool. "The body's a piece of plastic foam carved to fit the skin."

Meg laid the fish on a display case. It was mounted on a narrow strip of wood which, she realized, would fit exactly the outline left on the wallpaper in her sewing room-bedroom. It was easy to understand why Mr. Larsen had been proud of his giant catch, but she was glad it had been moved out before she moved in. The fanged mouth gaped wickedly in the narrow beam of light.

"Now what?" Caleb wondered. "It looks the way it always did."

"Maybe your dad carved a message on it," Meg suggested. Her fear was gradually giving way to curiosity. "Let's look."

Caleb moved the light up and down the long shape. Then he turned the fish over and examined the back.

"Nothing."

"Maybe inside. Is there some way to open it up?"

"Of course not." Caleb sounded disgusted. "I told you, the body's a solid piece of foam. Besides, I wouldn't wreck the fish on the chance that—"

"Its mouth," Meg interrupted. "Shine the light into

its mouth." She was running out of suggestions, but she didn't want to give up.

They moved to the end of the display case and crouched down. Caleb pointed the light into the fish's mouth. Needle-sharp teeth guarded the opening. Beyond them were folds of hard, dry cartilage, and thick flaps that formed the insides of the gills.

"There!" In her excitement Meg almost lost her balance. "In the back, Caleb. Isn't there something in the opening where the throat ought to begin?"

Caleb started to reach inside the mouth, then drew his hand back as the teeth raked his knuckles. "You do it. Your hand is smaller."

Meg bunched her fingers to avoid the teeth and reached into the mouth. Her hand and then her wrist disappeared inside the jaws.

"Can you get it?" The flashlight beam shook, Meg noted. She wasn't the only one who was trembling.

"I think so. If I can just hook one finger behind it . . ."

She picked gently at the object. At last it popped into the fish's mouth, where she was able to grasp it. "Got it!" she exclaimed and dropped her find on the display case.

Caleb groaned. "It's just a scrunched-up wad of brown paper," he said. "The taxidermist must have left it in there by mistake."

Meg picked up the wad and began to unfold it. "There's something inside." She flattened the brown paper on the glass, revealing a small rectangle of white paper and a tiny tissue-wrapped package.

Caleb snatched up the paper and held the flashlight close to it.

"'Butler and Olsen, Fine Jewelers, Chicago, Illinois,'" he read aloud. "It's a sales slip. My dad's name is on it, and it's dated October 17, 1983." He scowled. "That was the week before he was killed."

"What did he buy?" Meg asked breathlessly. Her eyes were on the little tissue package.

"A ring, according to the sales slip. He bought a diamond ring for twenty-five thousand dollars." Caleb shifted the light to the package. "Go ahead. We might as well open it." Suddenly he sounded tired almost disinterested.

Meg unfolded the tissue paper. The ring was a wide gold band set with one enormous diamond that was surrounded by several smaller ones. The stones glittered in the flashlight's beam.

"It's beautiful," Meg whispered.

"Sure it is," Caleb agreed. "And it cost twenty-five thousand dollars. That's about twenty-four thousand more than my dad ever had at one time in his whole life." He took the ring from Meg and stared at it. Then he wrapped it up and dropped it, with the sales slip, into his shirt pocket.

"Come on," he said gruffly. "Let's put the fish back where it was and get out of here."

Meg's mind shrank from the meaning of the diamond ring. She held the stool for Caleb to mount and return the fish to its place on the wall, then followed him wordlessly back to the entrance hall.

He pushed the stool under the stairs. "Where else did the kids go this afternoon?" he asked, his voice strangely flat. "Upstairs?"

"I guess so. And I'm pretty sure they went into the room across the hall. That's where all the animals are."

"You can wait on the porch if you want." Caleb made it sound like an order. "I'll check around and be right back."

Meg opened the front door and slipped outside, grateful for the chance to be alone. The night air cooled her hot cheeks and raised goose bumps on the back of her neck. Somewhere, not far away, a door slammed, and a whistle cut through the silvery night. "Come, Brownie!" a man's voice called. "Here, Brownie! Get in here, you crazy old dog."

Lucky person, Meg thought. *Nothing to worry about except getting Brownie to come home and go to bed.*

She slumped down on a step and rested her chin on her hands. *A ring that cost twenty-five thousand dollars. A ring where no ring should be, bought by a man who didn't have much money.*

It just proved, she thought, that a bad day could always get much worse.

15

They were halfway home before Caleb started talking.

"He went to Milwaukee on business the week before he was killed. That's what he told my mom, anyway. And that's what she told the police when they came around. I suppose what he really did was take his half of the stolen money and go to Chicago to buy the ring."

Caleb looked old in the moonlight, twenty-five, at least.

"You don't *know* that," Meg protested. "Maybe—maybe he inherited a lot of money and was going to surprise you with it. Maybe—"

"Maybe you have a great imagination," Caleb interrupted with a bitter laugh. "Let's not bother with fairy tales, okay? Do you know how much money was missing from the bank? Just about fifty thousand. Do you know how much money the police found in my dad's buddy's bank accounts? Just about twenty-five thou.

Probably my dad didn't want to keep that much cash around, so he took his share to the big city to find a safe way to hide it. What's easier to hide than a ring? He must have thought that musky's mouth was the safest hiding place in the world." His face crumpled for a moment as he accepted the logic of his own explanation. "Let's walk another block or so before we go home, okay? I hate to tell my mom all this stuff."

They crossed Emerson Avenue and walked on, with only a quick glance down the block at the Larsen house. Someone was standing on the front porch; Meg thought it must be her father. He was probably thinking about Grandma Korshak, wanting to know how sick she really was and not wanting to know, at the same time.

Not knowing is the worst thing in the world.

The words rang in her ears, and for a moment she didn't know where they'd come from. Then she remembered. She and Caleb had talked about his problems the day they went to the bait shop together. Meg had said, *having people say bad things about your father must be about the worst thing in the world.* Caleb had disagreed. *Not knowing is the worst thing. If I knew for sure what happened, I'd know what to do about it.*

"Well," she said aloud, "now you know."

Caleb looked down at her, startled.

"I mean," Meg hurried on, "you told me once that the worst thing was not knowing the truth about your dad. I know you wanted the truth to be something else, but at least you don't have to wonder anymore."

"Terrific," Caleb said sarcastically. "My dad was a thief. Every bad thing people have been saying is true. That really makes me feel a lot better." He glared at her, but she noticed that his angry stride slowed a little.

Farther down the block, a tall, thin figure came from between two houses and crossed the street, whistling softly into the dark. *Someone else looking for his dog.* The tall silhouette made Meg think of the gray-haired man in her dreams.

"It's so strange," she said, "the way your dad showed up twice in my dreams. I wonder why."

Caleb shrugged. "I wondered, too. Now I don't care."

"But you have to care," Meg protested. "Your dad wanted us to find that ring, Caleb. He did everything he could to help us. He even—well, I *think* he made me point the flashlight at the musky. I thought *you* were moving the light, but you weren't even close to me. We have to figure out why he did that. After all, he knew your mom was a totally honest person who'd never keep something that didn't belong to her. And he must have known she'd raise you to be the same kind of person. So why did he want you to find the ring?"

Caleb didn't answer. The tall man came back across the street with a sheepdog bumbling at his side. Meg watched them go up the steps of a house and disappear inside. Downstairs, lights flicked off, one by one.

Her mind raced, trying to find the answer to her question. "You know what I think?" she said at last. "I think he must have been really sorry he took that money. For one thing, he didn't rush to put it in secret bank accounts the way his friend did, where he could have spent it whenever he felt like it. Instead he bought the ring—something he could hide easily while he thought over what to do next. And then he was killed in that accident before he had a chance to return the money." She took a deep breath. "I think he came back in my dreams because he wanted to make things right. He wanted us—you—to help him."

Caleb's silence continued until Meg thought she'd burst. They reached the corner and stood for a moment just outside the circle of light cast by the street lamp in the middle of the intersection. Impulsively, Meg darted to the center of the circle and posed on her toes, arms curved above her head.

"And now we have Meg Korshak of the United States," she intoned, "Olympic gold medal winner, in her famous ice-skating routine. . . ." She began swooping and gliding around in the light, leaping wildly, twirling, and pausing occasionally to bow in Caleb's direction. At last, following a particularly frenzied jump, she heard him chuckle.

"You're a strange kid," he said. "Really strange."

Meg "skated" back to his side and, after a final

breathless bow, examined him closely. The tight, frozen look was gone.

"Well, what do you think?" she demanded.

"I just told you. You're one very weird kid."

"I mean about the dreams—and about why your father showed up in them."

His face was somber. "You could be right, I guess. It's as good an explanation as any other. I just wish—"

"So do I."

They stood at the edge of the pool of light, looking at each other. "You know what I *really* wish?" Caleb asked. "I wish it didn't matter why he came back, or whether he was guilty. I wish I could just say, 'The important thing is, we have the ring. From now on it's our decision —my mom's and mine—what we do with it.'"

"You *can* say that," Meg encouraged him. "You can take the ring to the bank tomorrow, and they can get their money back. And you can stop thinking about who did what years ago. It'll be over—sort of."

"Yeah, sort of."

Meg knew he was thinking about Les Machen and the other gossips who would be happy to be proved right.

"The thing is," Meg said slowly, hardly knowing how the sentence would end, "the thing is, you're separate from your father. I know you love him and you're disappointed and all that but"—for just a moment she felt again the unseen presence that had been beside her in the Lakes Room—"your father was then and you're now," she finished, surprising herself. "You really are separate, Caleb."

The words sounded cold in the summer night. It was a chilling thought, being separate from your parents. Meg wondered where the idea had come from; she'd never considered it before.

"That's true, isn't it?" She tried to sound more certain than she was.

"Maybe," Caleb replied. "I have to think about it." He sighed, and then to Meg's astonishment he took her hand and held it tight as they started back toward Emerson Avenue. "Let's go home. We've been gone so long, my mom probably thinks Steffi made a mess of every display in the museum."

Separate from your parents. Walking hand in hand with Caleb made the suggestion seem a little more reasonable. She could be separate from her father, who said writing was the most important thing in the world to him, and who was starting a whole new life here in Trevor. And separate from her mother, who loved Bill more than Meg (although she tried not to), and who didn't mind using Meg to make her former husband's life more complicated. Meg knew these things were true, and the truth hurt. Yet she loved both her parents very much.

"I love them, but we're separate," she whispered,

trying on the idea for size. "I'm me, no matter what they do."

Caleb smiled. It was a small, kind of sad smile, but a smile nevertheless. "Talking to yourself?" he teased.

"Maybe." Her thoughts crowded in on her — new thoughts and new feelings she'd have to get used to slowly.

Right now she wanted to change the subject.

"You know," she said solemnly, "I have this problem. I can't decide whether to try for another gold medal in ice skating or work on something new. Like downhill skipping."

It wasn't very funny, but that didn't matter. They both began to laugh, filling up the night with hoots and giggles. Then they started to skate, two Olympic ice-dancers gliding gracefully along the sidewalk together.

Across the street, a porch light flared. "What's going on out there?" a woman's voice demanded.

Caleb cleared his throat. "We'll be okay," he called across the darkness, "as long as we don't hit thin ice."

And that started them laughing all over again.

16

"When you talk to the police, don't tell them anything about my dreams," Meg advised. "They won't believe you. Take my word for it."

"So what *should* I say?" Caleb looked perplexed. "If I don't explain how we found the ring, they might think I knew it was there all the time."

"Tell them the same thing you told your mom last night—that you were showing me your father's big musky, and we noticed something stuck in the mouth. It's the truth—most of the truth, anyway."

They were sitting on the porch swing, waiting for Mrs. Larsen to change from her uniform to street clothes. She had, according to Caleb, stayed remarkably calm the night before, when he'd shown her what they'd discovered at the museum. She had just hugged him, and wiped her eyes a few times, and then she'd called Mr. Crayhill, one of Trevor's three attorneys.

After that she'd phoned the hospital to request a

half day off, and at two this afternoon Mr. Crayhill was coming to pick her up, with Caleb, and take them and the ring to the police station.

In the bright morning sunlight, Caleb seemed like a different person. In spite of the seriousness of the errand ahead, he seemed relaxed. Meg felt as if she hardly knew this almost light-hearted boy.

"It's a funny thing," he mused, propping his foot against the porch railing to give the swing a mighty shove. "My mom and I didn't talk much about it last night, but I could tell she feels the same way I do about that ring. She hates finding it, and yet she's relieved that it's turned up. Crazy, huh?" He sounded pleased, as if it was easier to accept his own mix of feelings if his mother shared them.

The screen door opened, and Mrs. Larsen came out on the porch. "This shouldn't take very long, Meg," she said. "But if we're not home by five, Mrs. Tate will start dinner. Maybe you can keep an eye on Steffi while she's busy."

At the sound of her name, Steffi appeared in the doorway. "I don't need anybody," she said, glowering at Meg.

"You do need someone, as long as you wander away from the house without permission. And as long as you break into places," Mrs. Larsen said mildly. "Remember that."

Steffi made a face. "I won't do it again."

"You'd better not." Mrs. Larsen looked ready to say

more, but just then a gray sedan slid to a stop in front of the house. Instead of continuing the scolding, she gave Steffi a hug and started down the steps.

Caleb tapped Meg lightly on the wrist, then catapulted out of the swing. "Wish us luck," he muttered and hurried after his mother.

When they were gone, Meg patted the cushion next to her. "Come on and sit down, Steffi," she invited. "Let's not be mad anymore."

"I'm supposed to stay with Granny Tate," Steffi replied stiffly. "Every single minute."

"Well, okay, then. I just wanted to say I'm sorry I yelled at you and Astrid yesterday. I did it because I like you so much and I was worried when I couldn't find you." *And because I was scared out of my wits.*

Steffi's pout faded. "That's all right. I'm sorry I threw Teddy at you." She crossed the porch and laid a small hand on Meg's knee. "Do you know where they went?" she whispered, nodding toward the corner where Mr. Crayhill's car had turned toward Lakeview.

"They had an errand to do."

Steffi frowned. "It's special," she said. "Mama's acting funny, and so is Caleb. Do you know why?"

Meg was still searching for a safe answer when Mrs. Tate called to Steffi. The little girl hurried off, obviously not wanting to get into any more trouble. "I'll ask Granny Tate," she said. *"She* knows everything." She darted off, leaving Meg feeling lonely and not quite forgiven.

If only Rhoda were here, or Bill! She needed someone to talk to. Now.

The telephone rang, and Meg dashed to answer it. Bill had said he'd call this evening, but maybe he already had some news to report.

"Hi, kiddo. Want to go fishing?" It was Meg's father, sounding unexpectedly jubilant.

"Fishing?" Meg stared at the mouthpiece, wondering if she'd heard right. "Aren't you at work?"

"Slow day here," her father replied. "The boss says I can take off if I want to. And I want to. I feel like celebrating."

"Celebrating—why?"

"Because," her father said triumphantly, "I decided not to wait for Bill to call. I telephoned the hospital in Milwaukee myself, thinking I could talk to a doctor or a nurse, and the next thing I knew I was speaking to Grandma."

"You talked to Grandma!" Meg's heart thudded.

"I did. And she gave me the news—straight from the patient's mouth, you might say. She has a gallbladder problem, but it isn't critical, and they're going to treat it with medicine and diet for a while. If she isn't a lot better in six months, they'll think about an operation. But she says she's feeling good, and she's going home tomorrow!"

Meg felt as if a boulder had tumbled off her shoulders. "Oh, Dad, that's terrific! She's going to be okay!"

"Sure, she is. So how about it?"

"How about what?"

"About going fishing, Meggie! Do you want to?"

Meg glanced up and discovered Mrs. Tate and Steffi standing in the doorway, smiling broadly. Happy because she was happy.

"I'll be ready when you get here," she promised. She hung up the phone and ran across the room to wrap Steffi and Granny Tate in one big hug. "My grandma's going to be okay!" she shouted. "She's going home tomorrow."

"That's wonderful, dear." Mrs. Tate returned the hug. "We could tell it was good news, couldn't we, Steffi?"

Suddenly the loneliness was gone. Hearing that Grandma Korshak was better had the same effect as turning on a light. It made the rest of the world look different.

"I have to get my tanning lotion." Meg started toward the stairs and then stopped. "I promised to look after Steffi later on," she remembered. "Maybe— Steffi, do you want to go fishing with us?"

Before Steffi could reply, Mrs. Tate broke in with unaccustomed firmness. "Not this time, Meg. It's sweet of you to invite her, but I think your daddy wants you to himself. Steffi will stay home and help me, won't you, dear?"

The little girl looked rebellious, then resigned.

"Okay," she said. "I'm really a good potato peeler, but nobody ever lets me do it."

"I'll let you do it."

"But next time I'm going fishing with Meg."

"Next time will be fine." Mrs. Tate looked at Meg thoughtfully. The look seemed to mean something special, and Meg wondered what it could be. She wondered even more when Mrs. Tate came to the front door as she was leaving.

"Your daddy's a dear man, Meg," she said mysteriously. "I know you want him to be happy, dear."

When he finally told her, the words were said so quietly that Meg almost missed them. "Kathy Larsen and I love each other, Meggie. We plan to get married, and we hope you and Bill are going to approve. After you have time to get used to the idea, that is."

No thunder overhead. No earth-rumbling below. Just two people in a gently rocking boat, and an eagle circling over the nearest shore. Meg kept her eyes on the eagle till it settled into the highest branches of a pine tree. Then she looked at her father. In spite of his casual tone, there were little drops of perspiration on his forehead.

"We'll still be a family, kiddo. It'll be a bigger family, that's all."

"It won't be the same," Meg said. "You and Mama and Bill and me—"

Her father leaned forward. "I couldn't make your mother happy—you have to admit that, Meg. I'm very lucky to find a wonderful person like Kathy who's willing to take me the way I am. She hasn't wanted to set a wedding date till now, mostly because she's worried about Caleb. But now that you kids found that ring—well, she thinks Caleb's going to be okay." He reeled in his line, inspected the worm, and threw it out again. "Well, what do you say? About our getting married?"

"I guess it'll be all right," Meg answered painfully. "I mean, if that's what you want. Mrs.—Kathy—is nice."

"Great!" Her father mopped his face. "Wonderful! How will Bill take it?"

"He won't mind as much as I do." Meg knew that was true. Last night, thinking over what she and Caleb had discussed on the way home from the museum, she'd realized that Bill knew a lot about keeping himself separate. Rhoda did, too. Now Meg had to learn how to do it.

"What are you thinking about?" her father asked anxiously. "Let your old man in on it."

"I was thinking, the last time we went fishing I was sure you were going to tell me about getting married. This time I didn't expect it."

Mr. Korshak looked stunned. "Last time! You mean you guessed how things were with Kathy and me?"

"Sort of. Granny Tate knows, too. I think she even

guessed you were going to tell me about it today."

"She's a wise old girl. Kathy confides in her, and she knows that finding the ring makes this a lot easier for us." Meg's father leaned back and stretched his legs as far as the little boat would permit. "I feel great," he said softly. "Grandma Korshak's okay, and you're not upset about anything. Are you, Meg? How do *you* feel?"

"I'm glad you told me," Meg said. "Not knowing is the worst thing." She would have liked to talk about that some more, but her father was too excited to listen.

"Kathy likes you a lot, Meggie. In fact, she thinks you're terrific. We want you and Bill to come to Trevor for the wedding this fall. You will, won't you?"

The wedding. Her father marrying someone else. The absolutely final end to life the way it used to be.

"If you come for the wedding, Kathy wants to make you a dress," he coaxed. "She's a great seamstress, you know. She even showed me the material she'll use if you like it — beautiful stuff she's been saving for the right occasion."

"Yellow material?" It was easier to think about the dress than about the wedding.

"Right!" He raised his eyebrows. "My daughter the mind reader."

"I like yellow."

She could have told him that Grandma Korshak had seen the dress in a dream — a real dream — but she knew he didn't want or need an explanation. He just wanted Meg to be as happy as he was at this minute.

Tonight, she thought, she'd write long letters to Bill and to Rhoda, telling them everything that had happened in the last two days.

After that, she'd write to Grandma Korshak and tell *her* that it looked as if their secret windows were still working very well indeed.